SO LONG

SO LONG
LOUISE DESJARDINS

A novel

Translated by Sheila Fischman

Cormorant Books

So Long copyright © Éditions du Boréal, Montreal, Canada, 2005
English-language translation copyright © Sheila Fischman, 2012
This edition copyright © Cormorant Books, 2012

No part of this publication may be reproduced, stored in a retrieval system or transmitted, in any form or by any means, without the prior written consent of the publisher or a licence from The Canadian Copyright Licensing Agency (Access Copyright). For an Access Copyright licence,
jvisit www.accesscopyright.ca or call toll free 1.800.893.5777.

 Canada Council for the Arts **Conseil des Arts du Canada**

The publisher gratefully acknowledges the support of the Canada Council for the Arts and the Ontario Arts Council for its publishing program.
We acknowledge the financial support of the Government of Canada through the Canada Book Fund (CBF) for our publishing activities,
and the Government of Ontario through the Ontario Media Development Corporation, an agency of the Ontario Ministry of Culture,
and the Ontario Book Publishing Tax Credit Program.

We acknowledge the financial collaboration with the Department of Canadian Heritage through the National Translation Program for Book Publishing.

Library and Archives Canada Cataloguing in Publication

Desjardins, Louise, 1943–
[So long. English]
So long / Louise Desjardins ; translated by Sheila Fischman.

Translation of French book with same title.
Issued also in electronic format.
ISBN 978-1-897151-90-7

I. Fischman, Sheila II. Title. III. Title: So long. English.

PS8557.E7828S613 2012   C843'.54   C2012-902415-5

Cover photograph and design: Angel Guerra/Archetype
Interior text design: Tannice Goddard/Soul Oasis Networking
Printer: Trigraphik LBF

Printed and bound in Canada

The interior of this book is printed on 100% post-consumer waste recycled paper.

CORMORANT BOOKS INC.
390 STEELCASE ROAD EAST, MARKHAM, ONTARIO, L3R 1G2
www.cormorantbooks.com

for Léa-Mei Bellefleur

SO LONG

The Fountain Pen

EVERY NIGHT WHILE I did the dishes, my father would write in a small pocket diary. It was a ritual; he took from its velvet case a gold pen that he called in English a *fountain pen* and I thought that words poured naturally from its golden tip, like water flowing from a blue, inexhaustible spring. I didn't know what he was writing, but I liked to see the letters taking shape, very upright, a rampart against the rest of the world. When he'd finished writing he would pour himself a hefty scotch and down it, To warm up, he said. Then he would bring his violin to his shoulder, run the strings of his bow through rosin, play an *a* on the piano, adjust his strings and take off into a phrase of Schumann or Rimski-Korsakoff that could break your heart — "Traumerei" when he was sad, "Hymne au Soleil" when he wanted splendour. He knew that my mother forgave him for nearly everything: playing his tunes too softly at the Look-Out Country Club; flirting with the pretty singers from Montreal; losing track of how many scotches he'd drunk; disappearing into the night without even saying goodbye, then coming back to life the next morning, grumpy and staring at his cold coffee.

After Papa's funeral last August, I nosed around in the notebooks he'd piled up in Mama's old cedar chest. I hoped to unearth some treasures, finally grasp what went on inside his stubborn head, put myself in touch with his soul, but I only found facts: weather, his small expenses, the number of hours spent at the Look-Out playing his violin. That's all. When he didn't spend anything, which was often the case, he only noted the temperature. He appeared to me the way I'd always seen him: tight-fisted, a man who loved scotch, feckless. He was the James of his private life, very different from the James of the Arntfield Country Club, a talkative James making sheep's eyes and smiling irresistibly; Jimmy to his friends, a nickname that startled me. At the grocery store, for instance, Madame di Sasso, Tony's mother, never missed a chance to tell me, You're lucky, Katie, you have such nice father. Such good-looking man. Oh, I like Jimmy playing violin. I would grit my teeth, think to myself, How can a Scrooge become a Jimmy?

Papa was quite well-known in northeastern Quebec, at the Ontario border, because of his store, the MacLeod Music Store, and his talent as a violinist. He was part of the Look-

Out Orchestra and also the regular accompanist for singers from Montreal, Toronto or Chicago. Female singers in particular, on whom he tried out his charms. Women, women, women — my father would have liked to possess them all — all the beautiful young ones. Mama, he didn't see anymore. She worked in the store selling records, making up orders, putting away the scores that music-lovers in search of a forgotten title were constantly shifting. My mother, plump and smiling, always ready to wait on customers. My father, who would criticize her for always wearing the same skirt, the same white blouse, would tell her when he'd had one too many, You've lost your gracious complexion, Gracia. Mama would retort, My customers like me, just ask them.

My mother died five years ago and I was never able to know what she really thought. I asked myself all the time, Does Mama really love Papa? Like me, she was probably afraid of him, of his fits of rage, but she couldn't live without his music. Playing the violin was like breathing for him, and because of his amazing talent for taking us to another world as soon as his bow slid over a string, she probably loved him in her way. Music brought them together. Some Sunday evenings, when he launched into "Greensleeves," Mama would get up from the table, eyes sparkling, chin up, to sing the old English song. My brothers and I would be silent, waiting for her to get to *Greensleeves was my heart of gold*, when we would join in. My father would stop short and declare, Katie, you're singing out of tune.

All right boys, let's go back to the chorus with Gracia.

My father was crazy about women singers, about the Quebec singer Alys Roby in particular, whom he'd accompanied at the Look-Out. He carried on until finally my mother, exasperated, yelled at him, You should have stayed single, not married, not had children. He replied, My mistake, Gracia, was leaving Scotland. Mama corrected him, You left Aberdeen, James, because you were poor and you wanted to find gold. That's why you came to Arntfield. To walk on gold. My mother took shelter in her bedroom, crying, and my father charged outside. I wanted to console her, but a little voice inside me told me not to budge.

My two brothers weren't allowed to go to the Look-Out, a huge building with many windows and imitation brick siding perched at the top of the village. A genuine castle out of *Jane Eyre* that only lacked a big English garden battered by Gothic winds. And like every fictional castle, the Look-Out had a history that had been told a thousand times. My mother used to say that some time in the 1930s, on the very night it opened, a woman had set fire to it. To punish her husband whom she'd forbidden to set foot there, that woman, according to my mother, speaking to my father in a quavery voice, that woman, she repeated, had waited for the last customer to leave, then she'd poured kerosene around the building and struck a match. Before the locals had time to wake up, the Look-Out had been reduced to a heap of ashes. Silence.

But the owners of the mine knew that for gold to spring out of the earth, miners had to be supplied with alcohol, music and women. And so the mine owners grouped together to rebuild the Look-Out in the same place, at the very top of the village, with its uninterrupted view of the Kekeko hills. Sometimes in the early hours of morning, my mother would have been happy to strike a match, too, so that it would be over, so that James no longer had to come home, so that she wouldn't have to wait for him anymore.

Our father's entire life was centred on the Look-Out. It was as if his day had no meaning until the moment when he stepped out of the house, alone. My mother had gone there only once, when the whole family had given a performance during the first part of the show by the popular comics, les Jérolas. I must have been twelve or thirteen; my mother and I sang, accompanied by my father on the violin, my brother Pete on guitar and my other brother, Don, on piano. That night, after the final words of the refrain, *Greensleeves was my heart of gold, /And who but my lady Greensleeves*, when the people in the big auditorium recognized the music from the popular TV show *Le Survenant* and whistled along happily, I promised myself that I would become a singer, like Alys Roby.

There were no other Saturday nights, that was the one and only performance by the future von Trapp family of Arntfield, Quebec. Something serious had happened because of a tipsy woman in a low-cut dress whom my father had kissed on the lips. It was to thank her, he apologized. My mother, furious, had hurled at him, Thank her for what? He couldn't answer her. He spluttered, Thank her for being there. My mother turned on her heels, head high, swearing that never again would she set foot in the Look-Out, even forbidding us to go. You have to pay attention to what Canon Fugère said in church, she kept telling us. It's a disreputable place, everyone there is drunk, it could catch fire any time. In fact, it had already burned once, it was set on fire by a woman who'd forbidden her husband to go there. Pete, Don and I looked at one another, sighing, Oh no, not the fire at the Look-Out again!

Despite the prohibition, I went to the Look-Out every day. I would leave home through the store, pretend to hang around and check out the display window for a while, then go off in the direction of the train station; I would walk past the closed boutiques, the bank plastered with posters, the old pharmacy, the pool hall. I stopped at the grocery store to say hello to Madame di Sasso, always neat and tidy with her plump chignon and her apron, Oh Katie, like a sun with your beautiful red hair, do you want something? No, no, Madame di Sasso, I just wanted to drop in and say hello. Then I would take off in the direction of the Look-Out, dragging my sandals in the powdery gravel, looking behind me to see if I was being followed. As I was circling the building I looked closely into the big dance hall. I had to get up on the roof, an easy feat for me because I was in the habit of climbing inside the elevator cages and trestles of mine shafts that overlooked the fields of slag. One afternoon I saw through the window of the bar a singer on her knees in front of my father, with her arms around his waist. I told myself, If only they would go away together we'd be rid of him, we'd have peace, blessed peace. I wished I could report to my mother what I'd seen; but, as relations between them were already stormy, I didn't.

One day when the Ink Spots came to sing in Arntfield, my father was on cloud nine. He invited them to the house without telling my mother. They filled up on scotch and left via the back door. I thought to myself, Mama would be furious if she could see those black people in her kitchen. Mama called them *niggers* and always pronounced the word *nigger* with a kind of disgust, as if she wanted to spit up some food. I think they're pitiful, she justified herself, because the whole world hates them. Their skin is so black. So don't you show up with a *nigger*, she warned me, or I'll ... As for my father, he was perfectly at ease with the Ink Spots. Their tours — that took them everywhere, from the Grand Ole Opry in Nashville to the Mocambo in Val-d'Or and the Club Charlebois in Rouyn — fired his imagination. I wished that he would go far away, but I knew that he dreamed of going back to the mines. He used to say, Over my dead body, I'll never leave, we're walkin' on gold here, they'll re-open the mines again some day — the Aldermac, the Wasamac — and I'll be rich. And me, in my little head,

I was thinking, Such stupidity, staying in a village up here in the middle of nowhere. We may be walking on gold; but, even if it's pure, you can't eat it.

I often wonder if my father was capable of loving anyone but a pretty young singer. When I was a child I was sure that he hadn't loved my mother for a long time and that my brother Don, who never thwarted him, was his favourite son. Don listened, uncomplaining, to his oft-repeated stories as if each time were the first. James loved my brother Pete as well, because he had a gift for the guitar. On one hand, he encouraged him to become a musician, to embark on the ambitious career for which he himself had lacked the courage, but on the other hand, every time Pete had a little success my father would rebuff him. You old fool, Pete would retort as he sneaked away. You're just like a fish, Papa would yell at him, you haven't got a heart!

Nothing has changed basically. That's what I told myself yesterday as I jotted the remark in my journal. It's true that for James, Pete was still the lady-killer musician, and Don the serious family man married to Sharon McCoy, our Irish girl from Nova Scotia. I searched in my memory for a time when I might have felt that my father loved me, but only one scene comes to mind: I am twelve years old, I'm in the Youville hospital in Noranda. It's night, I ask the nurse to call my mother, but it was my father who arrived a little later. He doesn't say a word, he squeezes my hand for a very long time and eventually I go back to sleep. The next day my fever has dropped and the day after that my mother comes to take me home. Never again did my father take my hand except for last summer, on his hospital bed, just before he died. How's Tony? he asked.

I don't know why he mentioned Tony, probably because he was still angry with me for having left him. I'd known Tony di Sasso since I was an innocent child, and after Monsieur di Sasso shut down his grocery store on rue Principale, I didn't see Tony again for ages, until I saw him again in grade eleven at the Noranda High School. I fell madly in love with him. One day I waited for him after school to meet up with him "by chance" and when I was alone with him I pulled out all the stops, You look exactly like James Dean in *East of Eden*. Tony, who was hesitating between becoming James Dean's double and gyrating his hips like Elvis, complete with tight jeans, slicked-back hair, took my words right in the heart. Later, we went out together for more than a year, making love every chance we got — in the bushes, in the graveyard, at the dump. It was a bombshell, for the di Sassos as much as for the MacLeods, when we announced our hasty wedding and our departure for Montreal. Everyone, with a knowing smile, assumed I was pregnant, which was absolutely true. It took a lot of persuading to make my father play his violin in the church, You can't be serious, I don't believe in anything, but he gave in to avoid tarnishing his image, to please Julia di Sasso, Tony's lovely mother, and he'd repressed his anger for a long time. Gradually, over the years, James had developed a soft spot for Tony. You're just like me, he would tell his son-in-law, which made me laugh. As tall, pale and thin as my father was, his nose aquiline, hair sparse and unruly, Tony was on the fat side, stocky and he took great care of his thick and glossy black hair. Later on, much later, I realized that James was right, I conceded that I'd married a replica of him: the same penchant for scotch and for pretty young women, the same friendliness towards strangers, the same irritability, the same stinginess with the slightest details of everyday life. I was very relieved when just a few days after my wedding, a big brownish clot fell into the toilet. After that I took the pill, very proud of having deceived those who'd had to stop their calculations after the prescribed nine months.

My brothers followed me and left as well, but in a brilliant move, they went to live at either end of the country, Pete in Vancouver, Don in Halifax. Coast to coast. I then was the closest to the family house, even if Montréal is more than six hundred and fifty kilometres from Arntfield. For my parents though, I was never far away, and I often made the return trip, especially at the end when my mother took sick. My father never stopped reminding me, We gave you a lot, isn't it normal that you should pay us back?

Don and Pete had a gift for creating something rare. They only turned up every four years and every time, it was an event. My mother would turn the house upside down to prepare for their visit, muttering as she cooked her tourtières and stews, Donald and Peter (she never used the abbreviated form of their names) are so far away. When they come to see me it's a gift. Then she would go over the family in her mind, I've lost my sons, I know practically nothing about their lives, Sharon is a nice girl but she's Irish and she cast a spell on my Donald. He's shrivelled up since they got married, though he used to be so pleasant, so happy. And their little William, my only grandson, I hardly ever see. And your girls, Katie, they don't come to see us anymore. Your daughters, such nice girls. Then Peter, my poor Peter, my bachelor son, always hard up, who turns up flanked by a different girl every time. *Always broke and never alone*, that was how Mama referred to her favourite. And she had trouble keeping the names of Pete's girlfriends straight, confusing Julie, Shirley, Joanne, Karen and the others.

Yesterday morning I thought about my mother who used to call me very early on my birthday. Occasionally she'd call at seven A.M. I wanted to be sure I'd catch you at home, she would say. I thought about François whom she would never know, François with whom I have a date for the first time. Then, opening the new exercise book that would serve as my journal all year, I also thought about my father, my father as he used to be, during my childhood. I took his fountain pen from its velvet case and wrote: *8 January 2000*. In the kitchen window I could see the snow fall, enveloping the day that was dawning. Then I wrote these dazzling words, which surprised me: *Katie MacLeod, Katie MacLeod.* My *name rings out like a candy apple. I am slim and beautiful, I am fifty-five years old. Today I am going to renew my life.*

Fifty-five, a strange number, often placed side by side with the word *freedom*. Freedom from what? From noting all the years gone up in smoke? What would have happened to me if I'd stayed there, in Arntfield, instead of going to Montreal to live with Tony? Maybe we'd have bought the Look-Out to turn it into a castle, bring up a large family, perform "Greensleeves" on Saturday night, entertain Oscar Peterson and Mario Lanza, become *artistes*. Maybe I'd still be with Tony, maybe my daughters wouldn't have gone away. Maybe the Look-Out wouldn't have burned down a second time. Maybe the gold mines would have opened again — and the bank and the pharmacy and the grocery store. Maybe.

Scribblers

EVERY DAY I jot down in children's scribblers what makes up my hours — the books I'm reading, whether it's raining or snowing, calls from my daughters, my little discomforts, my weight practically to the gram. I'm afraid that someone will stick his nose into these plain, unvarnished truths that are not expressed out loud, so I pile my notebooks onto a shelf at the back of my closet. Yesterday, as I do every year on my birthday, I went there to flush out my notebooks one by one. I spread them on my bed to hold on to some at random, thinking naively that I'd be able to retrieve my past by reading them.

Immediately I found a page from the year following my split with René, a notebook crammed full, needless to say, and I read: *8 January 1992, Pete showed up this morning, a good Samaritan, but he couldn't convince me that happiness consists of checking off "single" on official forms. Pete was bluffing, I know he bluffs because his voice always cracks when he laughs. He does his best to persuade himself that he can get along without a woman but I know that deep down he'd like to find one in his bed every night, a cosy, comfortable woman surrounded by well-brought-up children.*

I see Pete again racing into my place to console me, I see him again holding a bunch of mimosas, he's slim like Papa, with long, light-coloured hair, the bracelet around his wrist a gift from his latest conquest. I had written on the day after his lightning visit: *9 January 1992, Pete doesn't think much of women, but his airs of an accomplished playboy are appealing. Pete is hiding something from us. I don't like things left unsaid in troubled waters. I like a clear gaze that looks me in the eye, that's not an opaque window. Papa sometimes looked me in the eye and all I could see was a wall of ice.*

After my father died, I thought that I would finally have peace, but everything takes me back to him. Last fall I stayed in Arntfield to clear out the house. There was nothing valuable in the apartment, as Papa had already sold off the objects that would have been of interest to my brothers and me. As for the store, it had stayed in exactly the same state it was in when the bailiffs had arrived after my father declared bankruptcy. On the board displaying the hit parade two 1972 hits were always shown, "Papa Was a Rolling Stone" by The Temptations and "My Ding-a-Ling" by Chuck

Berry. On the shelves lay some old 45s and LPs, metronomes, and the yellowed scores for "En veillant su'l perron," "Les Trois Cloches," "Love Me Tender," and "Félix Leclerc, le Canadien." When James came to his lair every day it was to check that everything was still petrified in the dust like an impossible dream that one clings to. Life went on through these unsold objects that slept like the gold beneath the soil of Arntfield. The gold that no one has taken is still there, maybe it will waken one day.

My father opened the MacLeod Music Store in 1944, a few months before I was born, when Arntfield's Main Street was rolling in gold, showing off its store windows from the pharmacy to the pool hall. My father wanted to get rich, and the store prospered for a while, thanks to my mother who took care of the daily tasks of house and business. My father did the books, that's all, and he never gave up his violin, treating it with kid gloves, like his car. It was with that violin that he'd won over my mother, at the Swastika marshalling yard. While they waited for the train, he'd asked her where she was going and she had replied that she was going to Arntfield to teach in a small country school. As for James, he told her that he was Scottish, that he'd fled the poverty of Aberdeen to work in the Aldermac mine, also in Arntfield. By the way, you're a musician? asked Gracia, who was fluent in English because she came from Haileybury in Ontario. My mother had always sung in the choir. She would have liked to play the piano, but Grandmother

Michaud couldn't afford to pay for her lessons. And so, since she didn't play an instrument, she admired musicians. When Papa and Mama got married in Haileybury the summer after they'd met in Swastika, it was the first time the Michaud grandparents had met their son-in-law. The welcome had been chilly at first, everyone having noticed that my father did not kneel in church, but later, when they'd had a drink or two or three, the atmosphere warmed up. James had won the affection of the whole Michaud family by making the guests dance until all hours. No one came from Aberdeen, as my mother said when she was finishing the story of her marriage. Then she would look at my father and sigh.

My father and my mother lost their jobs at nearly the same time, just before I was born, but not for the same reasons. The Aldermac mine shut down, whereas my mother was fired because she was in the family way. As soon as she became pregnant a woman had to stop teaching, guilty of having sinned in her bed — that was what my mother said every time she found out that a woman was expecting a child, and she added, Times are changing and it's about time!

During the years when Don, Pete and I were very young, my mother stayed home, but as soon as Pete started school she felt she had to get involved in the store. My father wasn't very good at ordering and inventory, he preferred being on the road during the day to sell musical instruments, and to play the violin with the Look-Out Orchestra nearly every night. The hours dragged on for my mother, but she would close the store and climb up to our apartment and eat with us. She was an ambitious woman who would have liked to be rich, very rich. She didn't say so right out, but when she was going through her *Vogue* or her *Woman's Day*, *she praised the celebrities who'd started out with nothing,* who'd surmounted every obstacle to break through, to become somebody, make a lot of money. The 45 rpms of Jimmy James and His Candy Canes, Elvis Presley, Fats Domino, and Patsy Cline sold like hotcakes. People came from all over, from Rouyn, Ville-Marie, Kirkland Lake, to buy the latest hits. Often customers asked for records of which they could only hum the tune. My mother would listen to them very attentively and at the first notes she would wink at them as she went to take the record from one of the thousand small compartments behind the cash register. Every time she would savour her victory, closing her eyes as if she'd just won a trophy.

Upstairs in the family apartment there was absolute disorder. As my brothers and I were alone most of the time, we ate in the living room, in our bedrooms — everywhere. Plates could dry on a stool for days at a time before I picked them up. For doing laundry on the weekend, I'd collect clothes from all over and once they were clean, I would toss them in a heap into a big basket where everyone helped themselves. My father wasn't interested in the everyday details of life and my mother didn't have time to put things away. No one did it but me — now and then. What saved us was that once a year, in the spring, my mother hired two Polish women to wash the walls, the ceilings, the cupboards. They would spend two days with us. My father stayed in the house to encourage them and when they were finished the whole house was nice and clean. Life could begin again in its perfect disorder.

In the morning, my father would hang around the house, quietly recovering from the excesses of the night before, and in the afternoon he would climb into his car, his sample case under his arm, to look for customers. Evenings, he'd come home somewhat smashed, say not a word and shut himself away in his storage room, making out invoices to "collect" from his customers the next day. When he'd sobered up a little he would fix a meal just for himself, leave his dirty dishes in the sink, write in his journal and set out for the Look-Out. I felt responsible for his dishes even though no one ever asked me officially to do them. How I had reached the point of being my brothers' mother is still a mystery to me.

Some nights, my father would come home in a very good mood, especially when he brought along some musicians. He was very funny and affectionate then. Pour us another scotch, Katie. I was fond of my father when he played the violin or when he entertained. I'd have liked him to stay that way, drunk and lethargic.

Even after my mother's death five years ago, James went

down to the store every day. One morning last July, he didn't come back up but he'd had time to press the alarm button that he wore around his neck. The ambulance took him to the hospital where he stayed for over a week, half-conscious. I rushed to his bedside, spotted him behind the curtain, curled up. How's Tony? Those were his last words. I stayed alone with him for a long time and he looked at me gently with eyes blurred by morphine. His glycerined lips pronounced clearly the phrase *thank you*, I'm sure of it. At the moment when he could have told me at last that he loved me, the resuscitation equipment stopped. I kept his inert hand in mine, I rubbed his palm so much that it felt warm. His big body seemed even more emaciated, his white hair standing on end, something like the style affected by young punks. He's repented, I thought to myself, the old Scrooge. Then the nurse came in and murmured, It's over. She removed his tubes and he lay there with his mouth open, as if he were finally going to say the words that I'd been waiting for since my birth, My dear Katie, my lovely Katie.

This year was my first Christmas without my father. I didn't write anything about it in my 1999 journal, it was too sad. I was alone, my daughters wouldn't arrive until New Year's Day. I'd trimmed my Christmas tree, a genuine fir that drops its needles, which we have to pick up in every nook and cranny until spring, and I spent the day gazing at it like a little girl. I didn't cry, which surprises me. Sandra and Claire called, sorry that I was alone for Christmas. No, no, I told them, don't worry about me, I'm perfectly fine, it gives me a chance to rest. My friends Violette and Martine tried to persuade me to celebrate the Christmas Eve Réveillon with them and their families but I preferred to let the hours go by, haloed by the lights blinking on the tinsel garlands.

Abandoning the account of Pete's visit in 1992, I took my 1991 journal and got back into bed to plunge back into my reading. *9 January 1991, day after my birthday. Bright sunshine, -20C. What a horror show, if I'd only known! My old boyfriend Noël, my transitional lover, my candy man, the one who made me forget Tony and prepare for loving René, phoned the day before yesterday to invite me up to the Laurentians. We haven't laid eyes on each other for ten years. It will be your birthday present, he said, and I congratulated him for remembering. For my part I remembered that in fact Noël was born on Christmas Day. I thought he was intending to celebrate our birthdays and I equipped myself with candles and small presents. Turning onto the autoroute he stated quite casually that he felt totally free because his wife had just lost her father and had gone to Europe for his funeral. I said, Ah! The rest of trip he didn't utter a word, letting the hang-glider voice of Klaus Nomi fill the silence of the glittering landscape before us.*

As soon as we arrived at his house in Val-David, Noël got the big woodstove going and while we waited for it to heat up we inched our way beneath the matrimonial quilt to make love between two tokes. Then I brought out my little presents. Noël, slightly uncomfortable, barely looked at them and quickly prepared a plain vegetarian supper that we ate without appetite. Then under the quilt again to fill the rest of the evening. Yesterday, my birthday, it was past noon when Noël finally woke up. He drank his coffee without a word, then we went out to shovel the snow off the roof. We did some cross-country skiing. Night had long since fallen before he looked me straight in the eyes, and said:

"You're expecting me to wish you happy birthday, make you a little supper, give you flowers or perfume aren't you?"

"Um, yes, I guess ..."

"I'd better tell you right now, I hate birthdays. I don't wish you happy birthday, I didn't buy you a present, I haven't cooked a meal for you, don't expect anything from me! Do you want my toast and peanut butter?

"Well, umm ..."

"You like birthdays, don't you? The ribbons, the candles, the streamers — makes me puke."

Screaming like the damned, he turned on the television and I saw a drunk Elizabeth Taylor yelling at Richard Burton and throwing a glass at him. I lay down on a bed upstairs, wrapped in my parka, surrounded by stuffed animals in every colour and I didn't budge until this morning. I don't even remember if I slept but I do know that at daybreak, I gathered up my things and called a taxi. It cost a fortune but I was happy to go home.

I never saw Noël again. One day someone told me he was dead. I didn't even react, didn't think to ask if he'd gone up in a cloud of hash smoke.

I felt hot, I went to the kitchen to pour my fourth cup of coffee, then back to my room to pick up another notebook. Nineteen ninety-five this time. My mother died on the first page. All I wrote was, *She got to the end of her rope*, the rest of the page was blank. Poor Gracia, she was so sick that we wanted her to die. Very quickly she no longer even recognized me. Then everything deteriorated, she was confined to bed, she shrivelled up, refused to eat and passed away without making a scene, as if she had ordered the end of her life.

A few weeks before she died, I received an anguished call from my father, Come back to Arntfield as soon as you can. We have to deal with it, we have to deal with it, he repeated, his voice trembling. He had found her lying in the snow. Okay, Dad, I'll be there.

I stayed with them long enough to find a place for my mother in a seniors' residence. My father said, I know, I should be the one to do it, but I feel too old, too weak to commit her. She put up with me for so many years.

I did nothing to wipe out his guilt, I sometimes even added to it, reminding him how much Gracia had loved him, how she had defended him in front of us, her children, Yes, your father drank a little too much, yes, he's a tightwad, yes he's a penny-pincher, but he plays the violin and he's proud of his children. When he talks about you to his friends he describes you as geniuses; you should hear him. I grumbled, saying that he was only nice like that away from the house. According to my mother, my father was a *good person* but I couldn't believe her.

My mother fell asleep at any time, sometimes on the living-room sofa, sometimes in front of the TV, sometimes in her bed. I didn't recognize her then, she who had been so active, so vivacious, so vigorous. But I soon realized that it was an ingenious ploy in order to make herself impervious to blunders, oversights, humiliations. Flashes of lucidity would appear in her faraway look, then a wall of silence came down, as if she had temporarily left us.

Meanwhile, my father disclosed sotto voce some peculiar things about her, Can you imagine, Katie, your mother's gone crazy. She threatens to kill me, she wanders through the house naked, she throws out the TV remote, she wears a fur coat to eat breakfast. You can't imagine, Katie, it's unbearable. I don't know what to do.

He went on, terribly upset. I had trouble believing him, until the moment when my mother appeared in the living room wearing three skirts. She stammered, Sorry about my bathrobe, I can't find my skirt, where did you hide my skirt, James? I'll kill you unless you tell me where you hid the damn skirt. I thought, That woman, who's so intelligent, so rational, has turned into a selfish, untidy little girl and I did my best to calm her, Come on, Mama, sit down, you're just fine like that. My mother rocked in her chair, grumbling, James, you're plotting against me. James, you're cheating on me. I know, last night you went to Judith's place, you're cheating on me. I asked my father, Who is Judith? His only answer was to twirl his finger around near his temple.

Feeling distraught, I moved heaven and earth to get my mother into a seniors' residence in Rouyn-Noranda. When I took her there with her suitcase I had to lie to her, I'll come back and get you, Mama. You'll just have a short stay in the hospital because you're sick. You'll see, things will be better. My mother wept like a child who's been dropped off at daycare for the first time, I'm not sick. James needs me, I can't leave him all alone. I'm fine, I swear it. I don't need a rest, why are you so insistent? You're abandoning me. And where is James? Why isn't he with you? He's with Judith I suppose. He has shut me away here so he can be alone with Judith. I don't want to stay here, I want to go home.

I couldn't free myself from my mother. Briefly, I considered picking her up and taking her to Montreal. After all, Sandra and Claire had gone. Why couldn't she stay with me, on Fullum Street? I'd have made room for her in my bedroom. Then a nurse appeared in the doorway and seeing our two sorrows knit together, she said in a firm, calm voice, Don't worry, we'll take good care of your mother. She'll be fine here. Come, Madame MacLeod, come and rest.

I backed out of the small room that looked onto a snowy

garden at the centre of which stood a disused, decrepit rabbit hutch. From her rocking chair, my mother turned her back on me, staring at the window as she'd often done in the kitchen in Arntfield late at night, hoping that my father would come down the hill from the Look-Out. She muttered, They leave me alone in this strange bedroom. They've stolen my house, my kitchen, my store. I hate them all. It's unfair, doing that to me. For sure James is going to sleep with Judith. They're all ungrateful, the whole lot of them, my daughter, my sons. The lot of them. I want to die.

Once I was in my car I nearly went back to take my mother. Then the image resurfaced of Gracia coming into the living room puffed up by the three skirts on top of one another, wild-eyed. There's nothing else to do, I told myself. Mama died before her death, and I started the car. Fine snow sifted onto the road. Never again will my mother make this trip, I thought. I betrayed her, threw her onto the scrap heap like some worn-out thing. She is a defenceless fledgling I'm abandoning on the shore of a frozen lake. Do I owe her anything? Must I pay for having been a baby in her arms? Am I supposed to pay for that?

The tears were blinding me so much that I had to pull over onto the shoulder. I wished I could stay there, muffled in my sobs, not have to think anymore, telling myself that I had just lost my mother to her first death, the death of her mind, and that now I would have to wait for the slow death of her body. I got out of the car to brush off the snow and the damp air coming from deep in the Kekekos lessened my sorrow.

Stepping into the big run-down house I spotted James glued to the TV, holding a scotch, watching Dan Rather read the news. I asked him again who Judith was, why Gracia kept saying her name. His reply was, Never mind. I packed my bags in silence and left for Montreal that night. While I was crossing the railway tracks leading to Route 101, that Judith came back to me in a flash. Judith Ménard, whom people called the Countess of Farmborough, who'd been accused of setting fire to the Look-Out, which she owned. It was in June, 1972, and my mother had called me, shattered, Imagine, Katie, such a mess! I hope they'll lock up the countess. I'm sure it was her. Everybody says so, it will come out in the papers. And maybe your father will spend more time at home. What a mess, Katie!

The fire had created quite a stir in the parish of Arntfield. In court, the countess denied committing the crime. Appearances were against her, however: the Look-Out was falling into ruins and no one went there but the local mafia. I always suspected my father of making sheep's eyes at the countess, whom my mother was constantly making fun of. Everyone knows, she would say, that the countess is still thin and she still sings for her best clients ... James didn't move a muscle. Then, after the trial, my mother never mentioned Judith again except at the very end of her life when I committed her to a seniors' residence, where old people who've forgotten their names roam the corridors and rock themselves in the common rooms.

Two or three days after Gracia was confined, my father called me, I can't go to see her anymore, I can't do it, I'm sick. I want you to come up. And so I had to get a replacement at school, take a leave for the illness of a parent — at my own expense — and I came back, spending all my time looking after Mama, who spent a month in palliative care, curled up in the fetal position. I spent hours wondering if she was breathing, if she was thirsty, hot, cold. One morning, early, apnea won out over her breathing. It took a while for me to realize that she really had stopped living, that her breathing would not come back, nor would words or moans. I lay down beside her on the narrow hospital bed. I was at once so lonely and so calm that I could have stayed there for a long time.

Two days later, Don and Pete arrived for the funeral, which my father couldn't attend because of a terrible attack of gastric distress, vomiting all day and all night. Outside it was so cold that crystals in the air made breathing difficult. Aunt Gloria Michaud, who lived close by in Kirkland Lake, didn't come because of the fog. Only some of my father's old friends from the Look-Out had made the trip to share sandwiches and coffee in the church hall. Everyone agreed that Gracia didn't deserve that. Such a fine woman, so distinguished, so generous and intelligent ... No one deserves to die like that.

Orphaned now, I felt lighter and I lost my illusions. For me, no more Love with a capital *L*, no more stories about couples who go through obstacles the better to seal their lips together for all time. I wanted peace and quiet. I'm still good-looking in spite of my big hips, my small stomach and my chin which is trying to be double. Good looks mean nothing at all, my mother used to say as she put lipstick on her cheeks and back-combed her bleached hair. She did her best to be perfect. She would have liked to be more generous but how could she spoil her children with a grump of a husband who made a note of every penny spent? With the passing of time I think that my father killed my mother — as well as Katie, the little girl I had been, who would have been so happy to be her daddy's little girl. My childhood came back to the surface on a railway track that ran along highway 101, the Kekeko hills in the background, the gravel road that bends towards the Look-Out, where my father played the violin, where he met beautiful singers, where his life was lived, away from us.

When I put the journals back in my closet, the one from 1996 stayed in my hands. I don't have much longer, I told myself. I'm lost in my little old lady's memories, I have other things to do. But curiosity won out: another year, the last one, like a last cigarette before stopping cigarettes. I couldn't free myself from my life, from what had happened to me, and I opened the one for 1996 on January 9. This time it was about Marcel, a casual affair. Another one. *Yesterday Marcel took me to a little inn in the Eastern Townships. I didn't expect anything. I didn't even remember telling him that it was my birthday. Maybe I'd mentioned it like that, not making anything of it, during a conversation. Marcel had arranged with the cook to put a candle on whatever dessert I chose. I cried when he took a gift-wrapped package from his coat pocket. A piece of jewellery, insignificant. Romantic. Scared stiff that happiness was settling in. This morning before we left he was inattentive, vague. On the way home, he told me that he couldn't see me anymore, that his wife had found out about us, that she couldn't take it anymore, that he was going home, that he wouldn't call me anymore.*

Enough is enough! It struck me like a knife in a wound: the book of poems that Marcel had published and dedicated to his wife. Leafing through it I had recognized his passionate letters. Had his swarthy wife been aware of the marks on milky skin, on fiery hair? He used me to rekindle the dead desire of his dying relationship, I thought, but I will hold on forever to the soft texture of that weekend: the powder of mica dust in the fields, Marcel's hand on my knee, the mountains as far as the eye could see.

It was time for me to turn towards the future, to make resolutions. I put the page for January 8 in front of me and went on writing: *My auburn curls are barely streaked with grey. The freckles on my cheeks mask my wrinkles so well that people think I'm hardly forty and I take them on trust even though I know that things have changed. A slowness, heaviness, streaks — nothing to move me about my fate but I stay on the alert. For the time being I'm in great shape. Later on, if my morale should drop, I don't rule out a face lift.*

Then, making my way to the shower, I thought to myself, I'll write the rest when I know what will have happened to me today, 8 January 2000. Scrubbing my skin I was humming a tune of Michel Legrand's and thought of a remark that my grandmother MacLeod had written on a birthday card: *Happiness is like a cup of tea, with or without a cloud of milk.*

The Computer

MY LIFE UNFURLS in decades. When I left René Soucy ten years ago I gave him the house in Saint-Léonard, which I'd bought from Tony ten years earlier. Tony felt so guilty, he sold me his share for next to nothing. I did the same with René because the twenty years of memories accumulated in that reconstituted household were turning rotten. Since then, I've been renting apartments, each one smaller than the one before. Now I live in a three-room apartment — bedroom, kitchen, living room — on Fullum Street, on the edge of Plateau Mont-Royal, from where I can move any time. No more balance sheets, rambling, money problems. I'm not rolling in dough, far from it, I've given up even the thought of saving: columns of figures to manage, sums to invest — none of it interests me. I would rather let the money slip between my fingers, quicksilver. A way to take revenge on old James. As soon as I have a small sum of money I take care of unpaid bills, old debts. For years now I've been living off my line of credit, credit cards, overdrafts of all kinds. I have nothing, not even a house. How do people manage to hold on to their possessions? I lose everything, I'm careless. My daughters. My husbands. My plants. All that's left are some books, a few paintings and a whole pile of things brought home from travels.

And my precious computer that I'm plugged into every morning to read online newspapers, online horoscopes, online weather forecasts, to go to the online bank to transfer my online money from one account to the other. Then I turn to the Outlook email service in case there's a message from my virtual lover or one of my daughters. A loner's drug.

From Nunavik, where she teaches Inuit in a village school, Sandra emails me now and then, *Beautiful day, went out on skidoos, had fresh scallops, tired, love.* Sometimes she goes for weeks without replying but I keep writing to her regularly, as I do to Claire, who is studying sociology at the University of Mexico. Rather, *was* studying sociology, because her university is on strike. She doesn't even know if she will go back after Christmas. Actually I gave her *La Conjuration des bâtards* by Francine Noël for Christmas, a futuristic novel set at the University of Mexico that I'd read the minute it came out, to make me feel as if I was in the sun and the heat, close to Claire.

The much-dreaded apocalypse on January 1, 2000, didn't happen. Nostradamus and the merchants of fear were wrong — they who had predicted, with all the confidence of a used-car salesman, that computers would stubbornly not change at the start of the new millennium, that they'd turn into pumpkins on the stroke of midnight, that they hadn't been programmed to show a pretty 2000 on the screen, they couldn't go beyond 1999, proving that everything is transient in the Internet world where years are centuries.

Thumbing their noses at oracles, pacemakers still worked, and most computers, too. Mine didn't make a move — my laptop, my mailbox, nothing. Oh! I use it now and then as a notebook, at times of sorrow or terrible loneliness. When I was tending to my dying father, I was at loose ends while I waited for the end, and between visits to the hospital I wrote poems. I save them in files under a phony name, as if I were hiding them under a mattress. When I read them now it's hard to believe that I wrote them.

You shout yourself hoarse
On your barbed-wire stretcher
A slaughterhouse echo
Hot on my heels
Never old enough
To be old
Newborn
Shrivelled from swimming too long
In a woman's womb.

Again, old James, who haunts me still. Even his boring stories seem funny to me now and I tell them so often that my friends Martine and Violette roll their eyes as soon as I launch into one — as I did when my father recited the first words.

Yesterday afternoon I went to the Quartier Latin to see the film *Magnolia*. I was fascinated by the boy who takes part in a TV game show, *What Do Kids Know?*, who's fed up with being perfect. He holds back for so long to avoid annoying his father that he pees his pants. The film is full of stories about fathers who are the root of all evil. Tom Cruise is a perfect liar, because of whom? Because of his father, who abandoned him. The little budding genius is having a hard time, because of whom? Because of his father, who's too demanding. And the beautiful coke-sniffer is suicidal, because of whom? Because of her father, who abused her. Leaving the cinema, I asked myself, Why am I infuriated with my father? He never abandoned me, he wasn't too demanding, he didn't abuse me, he wasn't separated from my mother. Where does the intense anger come from that's gnawing at my guts six months after we buried him? When I was a child, where did the desire come from to be an orphan, to dispose of my father as if he were a splinter?

Did my daughters move away so they wouldn't need to kill me? I've never asked, but I hope that they don't want me to die right away. James never suspected how afraid I was of him. Did he ever wonder if I loved him or not? Maybe parents don't ask themselves that kind of question, are they so certain of being loved, in spite of everything?

Claire writes me often, more often than Sandra, in particular to ask for money. When I separated from René and his children, I upset the life of Claire, who was very attached to her half-brother Jean-François and her half-sister Marlène. I forced her to separate from them, from her father, from her beautiful big bedroom that opened onto a container garden of geraniums. Claire is angry at me for destroying her wonderful nonchalance. She tells me about it, makes me pay. And it works! Sometimes I have to borrow so I can help her out. I would never have dared ask my parents, who complained that they were the poorest people on Earth, for a cent. Be that as it may, when James died, he left a small inheritance shared by Don, Pete and me. That I in turn distributed to my daughters, not wanting to keep anything of my father's on principle, except for the gold fountain pen that I use every day for writing in my journal. I could have used the money to pay off my debts, take a trip to Europe, but I would have missed the vital insecurity that pushes me on, forces me to sort things out, to work, to do something with my life. One day I'll buy a plane ticket with my own money. I'll go to Scotland and try to find the ghost of James MacLeod on the streets of Aberdeen, try to understand why he put down roots in Abitibi.

A few years ago, I brought my computer to Arntfield and

suggested to my father that he visit the website of the city of Aberdeen. Looking at a gallery of old photos of downtown, photos from the twenties and thirties, he was impassive, but his face lit up at the sight of a beach on the North Sea. I went there once with my father and we ate fish 'n' chips. That's all he said. The light, at once harsh and misty, of the Aberdeen sky reminded me of foggy mornings when I looked out the kitchen windows, gazing at the Kekekos on the other side of the 101. I wished that James had talked about his childhood, his grandfather, his grandmother. Saying nothing, with a blank stare, he watched his TV news.

Sandra and Claire arrived safe and sound on New Year's Eve, taking advantage of big reductions on plane tickets because of the feared Y2K bug. Sandra and her husband, George, had left their baggage with Tony, who was still in love with his daughter and a little jealous of George, exactly as my father was with Tony. The long trip from Salluit to Montreal still inscribed on their snow-coloured complexions, they turned up at my place for Réveillon. Sandra hadn't come to her grandfather's funeral and I was now seeing her for the first time in more than a year. Her eyes shone, her black hair was longer, her cheeks more like apples. The Far North and marriage gave her a healthy look, put her feet back on the ground — she who drifted vague and diaphanous, always somewhat absent and dreamy in spite of her outbursts, her impulsiveness. It may be George who calms her, George and his almond-shaped eyes, his love for my daughter as vast and serene as Ungava Bay on a January noon.

As for Claire, she'd shown up all elegant and slim, accompanied by Silvia, a fellow student, fat and funny, who couldn't keep still, clamouring for everyone to dance the cha-cha-cha and playing over and over the CD of the Buena Vista Social Club. Claire would have liked the Réveillon to go on til dawn as they did when we were all living together — René, Sandra, Marlène and Jean-François. Mama, do you remember the house in Saint-Léonard, the Réveillons, Grandma singing and Grandpa playing the violin? They would arrive weighed down with fruitcakes. Uncle Don would play the piano and Aunt Sharon would sing "Greensleeves" with us. And our cousin Willie, who didn't understand a word of French, would try to follow our wacky conversations. And Uncle Pete would charm his new girlfriend, coaxing moans from the Hawaiian guitar on his knees. Those Réveillons were the real thing!

Around two A.M. Claire, droopy and dishevelled, wanted to pop another cork, Let's toast the millennium, let's toast the year 2000, but George, their designated driver, got to his feet, authoritative, That's enough girls, home to bed. George, who doesn't drink alcohol, Because of my genes, he says, didn't give in to the girls' protests. Claire and Sandra surrendered, reproaching me for having just one bedroom in my single's apartment, unlike their fathers, who have big houses. It's true, I don't have room for my girls, I don't have room for anyone. Claire staggered out last, turned around before she went down the stairs. I thought for a moment that she had something serious to tell me, but George called to her, Come on, we're freezing. I have to drive you back to your father's before we go on to Tony's. Tell your mother the story of your life when we come back for her birthday.

The following day, Sandra and Claire said, laughing, Fifty-five, that's something to celebrate, Mama. You haven't got a husband, you're alone, we're going to celebrate you, we'll take care of you. I've always hoped for and at the same time feared my birthday because it comes after Christmas when the people I'd like to ask over can't eat another bite, stuffed as they are with turkey, force-fed tourtières. *For your birthday and other feast days!* my mother would write on the card that came with my Christmas present. Then on my actual birthday she would stick a candle into the last serving of the *galette des rois*. Except for the one and only time I had a big party. I wish I'd been born in May along with the tulips, hyacinths and daffodils. But people can't be forced to celebrate and the older I get — let's say the word, *old — the more I don't mind people forgetting my birthday. I console myself as best I can because deep down I like to be celebrated too.*

Last year, on January 8 precisely, I sat for hours glued to the telephone. Charles, one of my former correspondents on the Open Heart Line who'd promised to take me out for dinner, hadn't even called. No sign of my daughters either.

I wasn't too surprised about Sandra, who was so busy, but Claire's silence surprised me: she always remembers birthdays and adores cakes, presents, candles, excitement, bubbly. I have my pride, I didn't call them. What would they have thought? Hi, it's me, your mother, today's my birthday. No, I kept my dignity and a lump in my throat.

So I celebrated my fifty-fourth birthday with my nose in a fat novel. It was François Rajotte, another correspondent on the Open Heart Line who'd urged me to read *Fall on Your Knees*, by Ann-Marie MacDonald. At the time there was no question of a love affair with François, but we had a shared passion for books and we both talked about what we were reading. In the evening, with my head still full of the Piper family from Cape Breton, I sent François a lengthy email, one that I keep in my "Winnipeg" file and look at now and then. After telling him that it was my birthday, I wrote, *First of all I was stunned at how much I shared with Kathleen, the heroine of the novel. Our first names were very similar — Kathleen, Katie; our fathers also shared a first name — James — and they were both musicians; Father Piper was a pianist while Papa MacLeod played the violin. As well, we both lived in a mining town, Kathleen's in Cape Breton, my own in Abitibi. But the differences appeared as I progressed in my reading. Kathleen was a tremendously talented singer, she'd studied in New York, while I only sang once in public, "Greensleeves," with my whole family. And then poor Kathleen died near the beginning of the novel when she secretly gave birth to twins. I read the novel uninterrupted, curious to know what else the author would cook up about Kathleen's death in such tragic circumstances. Closing the book I thought to myself, relieved, A novel is a wonderful thing, thrilling, but I wouldn't have wanted to end my days at nineteen while giving birth in an attic. You know, François, sometimes I'd like to transform, by magic, the deserted, dusty street of my childhood into a road at the end of the world that on some evenings merges with the sunset; but when I close my eyes and think back to Arntfield, I see only gravel, dilapidated houses, a disused train station. A trainload of ore that labours just as I'm leaving for school.*

Perhaps that letter was what set everything off. François replied promptly to wish me happy birthday, *I'd like to go to your place some day, see your books, meet you. I also had a sad childhood, that's one thing we can share.* I'd replied that I could quite possibly entertain him at my place some day. I regretted that invitation as soon as it was sent into the server's limbo. No way to get it back. Then I calmed down, telling myself that Winnipeg is far away and that Internet encounters never lead to much.

François was the only one to get in touch with me on the very day of that birthday in 1999, but the next day my voice mail was overflowing with excuses: Claire had a university exam, Sandra went back to Salluit that day with George, Sharon had forgotten to remind Don about my birthday.

Not a peep though from Charles, the other Open Heart Line correspondent, who was supposed to call me. So it goes. I'm used to it, I told myself. And he made so many grammatical errors ...

Life got over it and the next day I went out to eat with Martine and Violette, my old friends whom I'd introduced to one another and who'd become best friends. They've found that they have a lot in common and they often get together without me. They're both in their sixties, they're retired and live alone because it's been ages since their children were raised, educated, left home, got married, became parents. Like me, they are genuinely single. There's no one in their lives because as everybody knows not having a man in your life is the same as having no one.

It was actually on that January 9, chatting with my friends at the restaurant, that I made a resolution to find myself a lover, a real one. Yesterday, one year later to the day, I had a real date with my virtual sweetie. I hesitated before mentioning it because I felt that if I did, everything would fall through. For me, saying isn't doing. And so when I want something fervently, I don't talk about it. It was snowing hard and who knows, maybe the plane wouldn't be able to land and François would be stuck in Toronto because of fog. And so deep down, very deep and far down, I kept telling myself that I could simply not go, I'm free. But I can't play such a mean trick on someone who's flying all the way from Winnipeg.

Every time a message from Winnipeg came up on my screen, my heart beat faster. I didn't know if I was hooked on François or on his love letters. Yesterday morning he wrote to confirm, because he'd maybe sensed my uncertainty: *Darling, it's tonight that I meet Katie, my dear Katie who's been in my dreams for a year. I'll arrive at Dorval at eight p.m. Hope to see you there. Will I recognize you, with your green eyes, your red hair? I love you, darling.* I replied, *I'll be there, see you soon. I'll be wearing a black coat and a green-and-blue tartan scarf. You'll recognize me for sure.* I was incapable of adding, as he had, *je t'aime*, or anything of the sort. *Je t'aime* doesn't ring true. In English one can say *I love you* lightly, it doesn't commit you, it can just as well mean *I'm madly in love with you* or *I'm fond of you*, but when you write *je t'aime*, it's not the same as writing *I'm fond of you*.

The truth is that I had an irresistible urge to slip away as all my other Internet correspondents had done, zealous men who every time, after a long, humiliating wait, had let me go home empty-handed, alone and helpless. François is different, he's taking the trouble to come from far away. And Dorval isn't the Café Cherrier where, in no time at all, and quite invisibly, one can step inside the Sherbrooke Metro.

I clicked on my "Winnipeg" file where the life and soul of my future lover are preserved. Looking at that long list of messages made a burst of warmth pass through me from head to toe: I don't know a thing about him, I thought to myself, nothing but a few details, some vague likes. He enjoys books and films, he's refined, you can see that from his choice of words, from his well-constructed punchlines. My anxiety persisted. Would the real thing, in the flesh, be even nicer? A rendezvous is compromising. Of course it was written in black on white on my computer screen that we would still be free to see one another after this first encounter. I had insisted. Just before I turned off my computer I accidentally clicked on an old message from François, which I translated mentally as I read it, *You can't imagine, Katie, how much I need to see you, to touch you, to hear your voice, to smell your perfume, to drink the milk of your skin.*

We've barely spoken on the telephone, having decided to reveal ourselves mainly through the words that travelled across the Web, to leap into a net of acrobats of the heart. I placed all our exchanges in a binder, like love letters, without stamps or rose petals or perfume. It was all there in our correspondence — our lives, our moods, our lacks. Words, once written, are married, joined for life. My "Winnipeg" binder is an IBM version of love. How could true love emerge from a CD-ROM?

I hadn't slept with a man for four years. Marcel, at a little inn in the Eastern Townships, was the last one. Since then, I've found it more convenient to subscribe to the Open Heart Line. All my efforts at dating on the Web have failed, it's enough to make anybody feel down. Yet my message cast the net wide. *Redhead, full of tricks seeks male companion, any age, smoker or non*. Each date had been confirmed by phone, it seemed to be in the bag. Café Cherrier, corner of Cherrier and Saint-Denis, an address hard to miss. Guys get lost though ... Every one. I try to convince myself, Come on, Katie, shake off bad memories, the future lies ahead.

The day before yesterday, as seems to be the custom on my birthday, Martine and Violette took me out for dinner. They'd chosen the Symposium this time, because I adore fish. After we'd savoured some marvellous grilled cod and drunk two bottles of Chablis, we embarked on the big secrets. I admitted that "his" name was François Rajotte and that he was a few years younger than me. He's an Anglo from the prairies but, I felt I had to reassure our *indépendantiste* Violette, his name is very French and his sixteen-year-old daughter is called France. What does he do? asked Martine, always thinking about my precarious financial situation. I didn't know what to say; He's the host of a radio program, I said. Maybe he's unemployed, said Martine, not thinking. I replied that was not the case — without giving her the details she was expecting. A heavy silence hung over our fishbones. Violette cleared her throat and changed the subject, finally saying, Don't dither, Katie. This will be the right one.

Then Martine rhymed off her list of virtual lovers, her chatlines, which became more and more incredible as the *digestifs* touched down on the Symposium's checkered tablecloth. Summing up all her searches she looked like a jobless woman spieling off to an agent her latest steps in looking for a job. She finally confessed, thick-voiced, that she'd also had a correspondent in Winnipeg whose first name was François, which made me jump, You aren't going to steal my boyfriend? With her big spaniel's eyes she reassured me at once, Of course not, Katie, his name wasn't Rajotte and anyway, he hasn't written to me for a long time. He was too intellectual for me, all he talked about was the books he was reading and the films he wanted to see. She winked at Violette, which did nothing to set my mind at rest, and I wanted to be on my way. And then Violette said, taking a solemn break after she'd inhaled her cigarette, Girls, I've decided to stop computer dating because I've concluded that guys who sign up for Open Heart Line aren't interested if we're old or fat. It's fine if Rubens painted them, but they're out of style nowadays. I've come to terms with it. I added, And you're telling me to keep my date? What's going on? That was when Violette said, I want it to work out for you. What happened then was mind-boggling and as far as I'm concerned it's over now, but I'm an inveterate optimist. Violette launched into what she'd been hiding from everyone, even us, her two best friends. Maybe virtual broken hearts are worse than live ones, she began as a preamble, because you can't talk or write about your frustration to a lover you haven't actually met. Then she explained that she'd corresponded for six months with a Russian who said that he loved her very, very, very much. She'd gone to Moscow to meet him (so *that's* what her trip to Russia was about), they'd got married, then she came home long enough for the immigration papers to be in order. Anton was supposed to arrive in March but it was put off til April, then June. In the end she never heard a word from or about him.

That story was the coup de grâce and we closed the restaurant, to the great relief of the owner who'd long ago finished wiping his glasses. Violette and Martine wished me good luck which reeked of irony because of all our abortive dates and the weirdoes who'd slipped away. Don't push it, girls, I replied. There were moments of grace regardless, which encouraged us to go on, and on. Good gamblers, we burst out laughing as we strolled through the fluffy snow.

As soon as I was home I slumped onto my bed, thinking that this might be the last night I would spend on my own, not really believing what was going to happen to me: to sleep with someone who loves me, who has never seen the texture of my skin.

Lingerie

AT HALF PAST nine yesterday morning in the year 2000, as I did every January 8, I took a reading of my life. I'd showered and had breakfast and it was high time I got moving. I decided to go out and buy new underwear, just for the pleasure of imagining what would come next and I went out, muffled up in my parka.

After René and I separated, I consulted a psychiatrist whose office was next door to Holt Renfrew. When I left, shaken by my therapy session, I would console myself by checking out the elegant underwear department before I went down into the Metro, a matter of getting back some confidence in my powers of seduction. I decided to go there this morning. My dear Manitoban, I told myself, must prefer Anglo lingerie. Maybe I wouldn't even have to undress, maybe we'd only look at each other without even touching.

A peck on the cheek, that's all.

It was snowing little feathers again yesterday morning. My big Mercury was buried in an enormous snow bank and as I was ready to take on the world, I decided to try freeing it without using my shovel. I zigzagged, backed out, moved forward, first gear, a little to the right, a little to the left and finally I got out. I enjoy navigating in this car with its aeronautical dashboard. The doctor had advised James to stop driving, but he was wasting his breath, he'd chosen to put it away in his garage, giving it the same attention he gave his violin, stroking it as if it were a baby. Some summer afternoons he even took his nap in his darling Mercury, his soul, his gold, an unhoped-for refuge against the incomprehension of the universe. A few weeks before his death, he'd called to offer me his treasure. Take care of it, he told me solemnly, and remember that this car has never in its life slept outside.

Whatever James's beliefs, whether he is in heaven or hell, ever since the Mercury has been living in Montreal it has spent its nights under the stars — Tuesday and Thursday on one side of the street, the rest of the time on the other. Every time I drive it I have the impression that my father is spying on me from the back seat. Maybe he's laughing at me, maybe he's protecting me, whispering *Katie darling, take care.*

Against all expectations, I happened on a cleared parking space on Sherbrooke Street. My lucky day. My horoscope for that day explained that the moon was entering a good phase, that I shouldn't let myself be disheartened if I were tripped up by dark stars. I've never told anyone that every day, my horoscope offers reassuring words even though I don't believe them. After all, even though I'm an atheist I sometimes, when I'm very frightened, plead with God.

My footsteps sank into the snow and the gazes of the rare passersby turned towards me, gazes unknown and mute. He thinks I'm walking towards my happiness, I thought to myself when a man smiled at me. I spoke to him, Bonjour, Monsieur. I didn't know him and it hardly mattered. He could have been François and I caught the man's smile between his teeth. You have no idea, you who like me are walking in the dense slush, it's my birthday and I'm full of beans, I can take on the world. Why? Because I've got a date and in a few hours my daughters are going to celebrate me.

After I'd bought some lingerie that would lift my breasts and flatten my stomach, I intended to go to the hairdresser. Then, I told myself, I'd go home for my daughters' brunch. I was banking heavily on my hair to correspond in every respect to the photo I'd sent François via the Open Heart Line. My hair which cascaded down either side of my face impressed him. Not a word about the Mona Lisa smile that I'd worked on for hours.

Sandra and Claire wanted to celebrate at night, but I refused categorically, Not on Saturday night, girls, I'm busy.

They didn't insist but they persuaded me to let them celebrate my birthday over brunch at home. They would take care of everything while I was out. You shouldn't come back to the house before 12:30. I'd promised to obey them to the slightest detail, thinking that afterwards we'd go to Saint-Denis Street to track down a dress. It would be my day, a day devoted entirely to me, interspersed with hugs from my daughters. We may have time at the end of the afternoon to rent a film as we used to do, when we'd watch tape after tape, fingers sticky from popcorn, clustered with René and his children, Jean-François and Marlène, on the old basement sofa in Saint-Leonard.

A grey-haired saleslady approached me and asked if I needed help. Her white uniform and her east-end Montreal accent gave me enough confidence to admit, with my cheeks ablaze, that I was looking for lacy undergarments. She quickly pulled off the display racks a dozen brassieres straight out of a fashion magazine. I stepped into a changing room covered with mirrors to try them on. I'm sorry, but nothing suits me. My breasts spill out of the cups. The saleslady reassured me, Don't worry, I have larger sizes. A few moments later she brought me a package of flesh-coloured bras. I insisted, What I really want is lace, preferably black. She winked and came back, triumphant, Try these beauties! She felt my breasts as if she were performing a mammogram, then decreed, It's the right size and the lace is lovely. I answered, I need the matching panties so my stretch marks can't be seen. I've got just the thing, she murmured, going back to rummage in the shelves.

The displays were crowded with elegant negligées, meticulous and nearly puritanical. The icing on the cake. I thought about my mother and the washed-out, worn-out white bras she used to hang up in the bathroom. It wasn't important to her. Impossible to imagine my father and mother naked in bed, yet Gracia, so prudish, would parade around like Eve in the snow-covered yard in Arntfield. My mother had Indian skin as she liked to say, even though there are no known Indians on the family tree. The saleslady came back, That will be a hundred dollars. You made a good choice, congratulations and have a pleasant evening!

I wondered why she'd congratulated me, how she could have guessed that I had a date. Was the word *love* written on my forehead in letters of gold? I left the lingerie department, attracted by the plaids, the Scottish kilts, jackets, fancy scarves, unisex and universal. My MacLeod grandparents never came to Arntfield, I never saw them in the flesh, but in the sepia photo that was gathering dust on the piano, Grandfather wore a tartan kilt identical to the one that Grandmother MacLeod gave me for Christmas, red and yellow, green and blue. My little brothers got scarves, my father unwrapped his bottle of scotch. My mother tried to read the greeting card, *Would like to be with you all for Christmas.* It was out of the question that the grandparents leave their house in Aberdeen even for a week to visit their grandchildren, and for their part James and Gracia, even if they hesitated briefly when Grandfather MacLeod died, never travelled to Scotland. *Too expensive.* Much too expensive. Swigging scotch, my father talked to us about his mother, An absolutely gorgeous lady, witty and strong, then he switched to French, looking at me to tell us that she was authoritarian, cold and loathsome. You're like her, Katie. The same froggy eyes. And whenever I expressed an opinion, my father would put me in my place, nipping in the bud any chance of discussion. His mother, whom he'd run away from, had been reincarnated in his daughter — me, Katie MacLeod. I may go to Aberdeen some day. I'll never find out everything, but I'd like to talk with some cousins who'd known my grandmother. Yes, some day I'll go to the seaside in Aberdeen, a name that sounds like a delicate green to my ears, but not before my father has been deleted from my skin and my brain, not before I can think about him without a grain of sand scraping my palate.

Just before I went through the store's revolving doors, an old lady with trembling, purplish hands and a face that had been lifted to the ears, was spraying herself with Chanel Number 5. It was Mama's perfume. When Mama went out she would give the nape of her neck a single spray. She refused to lend me her futuristic atomiser. It was a gift from your father. As soon as she was out the door I would rummage in her drawer and spray perfume all over my body. I would plaster my mouth with lipstick. I'd have liked to add powder, eyeshadow, mascara, but she didn't have any of those. Too expensive.

One day, my father came in without knocking when I was trying to draw Marilyn Monroe's lips over mine. Bitch, what the hell are you doing there? And we were off. As he hit me, I saw a glimmer of sensual pleasure in his aluminum eyes. The red of the blood mixed with the greasy red of my lips and my tears. He stopped dead. For years I couldn't put on lipstick without seeing blood gush out. James may have felt badly about what he'd done, I have no idea. My mother tried to sort things out, to excuse him, saying that we had to forgive my father, that he couldn't help himself, that he'd been drinking, that he didn't know what he was doing. What my mother never understood was that, on that occasion, my father had broken me in two.

The first heavy snowfall covered the branches of the big trees and brought calm to Sherbrooke Street. Like an aisle in a cathedral. All at once I thought that François hardly ever spoke French, even though is name couldn't be more French. His mother is Anglophone, his father Franco, but at home they spoke only English. His mother had probably never in her life been able to produce a single u, a single rolled or fricative r. When James arrived from Scotland in 1937, he didn't speak a word of French, but things being as they were, he became bilingual. After my birth, Gracia had spoken only French to him. Marking her territory, I suppose.

In Montreal now one can have tea in French at the Ritz, shop at Holt Renfrew in French. I was carrying around the proof: a bag in which was curled up some embroidered black lace lingerie from France. And I had a date with François Rajotte from Winnipeg, whom I knew without having met him.

The window of a jewellery store was filled with gold crosses identical to the one that Gracia was wearing in her grave. I wondered if François practised any religion. And why we'd never brought up the matter. They're weird, mixed marriages, my mother so very pious, so Catholic, falling in love with a Protestant. The entire Michaud family had said novenas for James to convert. A waste of time, my father and faith weren't joined at the hip. James was always making fun of Father Fugère; of forbidden pleasures; of absolution without trial that the canon, from his confessional, granted to incestuous fathers; of the suffering and misery of the poor; of the fate of those who were surrounded by papal comfort. I didn't say so, but I more or less agreed with him. I assume that he wanted to provoke my mother who was tangled up in the great mysteries of the Immaculate Conception or the Assumption. In our family, Don is the only practising Catholic, because Sharon is. When I was teaching religion to the children I did it without enthusiasm, out of obligation, trying not to lay it on too thick, sometimes feeling that I was in the wrong.

I decided not to disturb my Mercury sitting up to its

ankles in a cozy nest of big, soft snowflakes where a grader had left it. It was already half past eleven and, as I made my way at a good clip towards the Peel Metro, I walked along Stanley Street, at once attracted and irritated by all the high-tech mannequins in the store windows, skinny as scallions, with identical faces regardless of whether they're men or women, some painted brown, others yellow. Despite the colour of their skin they have the same nose, the same lips as white people of the western world.

At the entrance to the Metro, big posters advertising Paul-André Fortier's show at the Agora de la Danse lined the walls. *PAF! 3 solos*. I took a seat next to a woman with a face so smooth it resembled a waxen mask. How old could she be? Her living hands were eighty, her funerary face suggested no more than fifty. I opened my *Devoir* and came upon an interview with Paul-André Fortier who admitted that he was performing again just for the pleasure of dancing, at an age when dancers no longer dance. To look in his past for the tracks that would lead to his future, to rediscover what he had to lose in order to go on. Lucky man, to be able to empty one's pockets, to lighten oneself through movement. I wished that I could learn to dance like him, to catch fire, no longer to feel my womb that was so heavy, so empty.

The Hairdo

AT THE PLACE des Arts Metro the cement walls are covered with posters for shows, but nothing tempted me because I could never get enough of being at home alone. When I stopped teaching last June I felt sick over all the reforms, the made-up gobbledygook to describe simple ideas such as knowing how to read, write and reckon. A huge fatigue took hold of me and in the end I ran out of patience faced with a foul-mouthed brat. The slap flew out on its own and I was the one who started to cry. The parents lodged a complaint and when the principal suggested I take sick leave, I told him, as if I'd been thinking it over for a long time, that I wouldn't come back. Early that summer I hung around, convalescing from thirty years of work, not believing what was happening to me. I thought to myself that I would take singing lessons, some day go back on stage and sing "Greensleeves" as we'd done at the Look-Out when I was twelve. I signed up for a choir, but when Papa died I dropped everything to plan his funeral and look after the estate. After the burial I lit a big fire behind the house to burn the old invoices from the store. Then I threw onto the fire boxes full of stars, angel stickers and loose sheets of paper, which I kept in my glove compartment.

Walking through the tunnel to Complexe Desjardins, I was breathless, as if I were carrying a weight that I'd never be able to drop. For a short time after René and I separated, I was euphoric, I was going to be sole mistress on board, I would be able to go out when I pleased without negotiating, to plan my own supper or when I went to bed. Over the years I'd weakened and gradually the urge to meet someone came back, hardly noticeable at first, like a pain one doesn't want to acknowledge, obsessive in the end, like an abscess that has to be burst. The Open Heart Line acted as a bridge and Léon maintained my illusions by doing my mop of red hair that had fascinated Tony di Sasso, René Soucy, Noël, Marcel and all the others.

When I murmur the story of my life to Léon, he listens and only interrupts to revive the confidence when it's liable to go out. He is one of those individuals who never forgets birthdays. As soon as he noticed me yesterday he called out affectionately, Not too down on your fifty-fifth, Katie? After holding forth, as only he can do, on the amount of snow on the ground, he quickly asked about my love life.

Directly to the point, as usual. He felt my hair, a forgotten singer's, lifting handfuls of it with his long, nimble fingers, assessing its weight, then letting it fall onto my shoulders. I'm still single, Léon, and it suits me fine. To worm the information out of me, he used his old tactic of rewinding, You didn't look that great when your Tony left you for a youngster. Oh là là! Cheap shot, Léon. What are you trying to do now? I forgot all that ages ago. But Léon didn't capitulate, I remember, Katie, you were angry, so furious that you wanted to change your whole body, dye your hair platinum à la Marilyn Monroe. It's true, Léon, you absolutely refused, you even told me to go and see someone else and I came home desperate at the prospect of putting up with my freckles and my red curls for the rest of my life.

Léon pressed my scalp in the right place, stopped where my brain was seething, sucked up a sip of coffee then went back on the attack, Are you all right, Katie? I'm okay Léon, I already told you. Dear Katie, I wasn't convinced, believe me. Tony di Sasso, I replied, was so long ago. It's true that he liked my hair ... Léon pricked up his ear to hear a next chapter that didn't come, and I closed my eyes. It's true, I thought to myself, Tony liked to stroke my hair, ruffling it as he whispered, Your hair is the colour of a larch tree in the fall. We were great together. Tony wanted children but I didn't, I had them by the thirties at school, renewable annually. After ten years together, I became accidentally pregnant. Tony was thrilled, I wasn't. All those years of keeping an eye on my brothers, of fixing their meals, had put me off motherhood. When Sandra was born, nothing happened the way it does in *Dr. Spock*, everything was difficult and I was nothing like a pale pink mommy in the nirvana of giving birth. To tell the truth, I was exhausted and depressed, unable to get up at night. I wanted to put Sandra in a day nursery for a few days but Tony wouldn't hear of it. As I was crying non-stop he took the baby to his mother, who had come to live in Montréal-Nord after her husband's death. Madame di Sasso had said, Tony repeated it often, that I didn't have a heart. With her accent à la Sophia Loren she called me every day, I wonder how you do it, Katie, not to be closer to your daughter, the wonderful little Sandra. She's so adorable with her black hair and her lovely dark eyes. She's a di Sasso all right, she'll have a temper like her grandmother Julia. And she's your first child, after all!

She finally got to me and I asked Tony to bring back my daughter. Something was broken between us. Siding with his mother, Tony had betrayed me. All the love and all the affection now went to Sandra. I tried hard to persuade myself that I was a good mother and I wrapped myself so tightly inside the cocoon of my daughter that Tony became a stranger to me. Then Sandra started sleeping through the night, she walked, talked, grew, began to defend her territory, to express an opinion, to resemble her father more and more. Tony took his distance from her just as he had gradually loosened his ties with me. He loved the baby doll, he couldn't bear the complex human being Sandra was becoming. You're conspiring against me, he would say. And what had to happen happened. That Friday in May, 1980, is still intact in the skin of my memory.

The final hour of visual arts couldn't calm my swarm of thirty little minds and when I went inside and put down my briefcase full of notebooks to be marked, I saw my drawn face in the hall mirror before I noticed Tony deep in conversation with the babysitter. So, I thought to myself, Tony is home early. My Bonjour, everybody! tossed off as I opened the door got no reply and when I sat down at the table with them, discomfort contaminated the silence. Tony hesitated and then, before he could make a sound, I shouted, Is something wrong with my baby girl? You're hiding something from me. Where is she? Tony reassured me, Sandra is playing in the garden with her friends, don't worry about her so much, Katie. So it's you, Tony, you've been fired from the garage? Again Tony told me not to panic, it wasn't all that serious.

Tina looked down, then Tony removed from his leatherette briefcase a big sheet of paper, eight and a half by fourteen, which he unfolded cautiously before my eyes. In big letters was written, *Granger and Granger, Lawyers. Consent to judgment. Applicant and respondent will have shared custody of the minor, Sandra.* I could not believe what I was seeing. The words danced before my eyes, the paragraphs were all confused. I said, Sandra, Sandra, Sandra. Tony assumed his salesman's voice, Don't get worked up, Katie, I'll have Sandra with me every other week, everything will be divided equally. What I'd just learned in five minutes didn't make its way into my head. I was the victim of a plot, I'd been betrayed, murdered. I burst into tears. You should have talked to me about it, Tony di Sasso! How long has there been someone in your life? Tony took a look burning with desire at the babysitter and the doubts, the insinuations, the equivocations I'd been trying to smother for several weeks overwhelmed me. I slammed the door and I saw Sandra playing in the garden with her friends. She told her doll, Go to sleep, be a good girl, Mama's going to come back. Sandra's black hair, my child's, floated in the sun, stood out against her white T-shirt. She came up to me, worried, Why are you crying, Mama? I took her hand and led her into the house, Come with me, Papa wants to tell you something, sweetheart.

Tony got up to go, Wait, Tony, you have to talk to Sandra. Tony's eyes were wet. He said tonelessly, Later Katie, when the dust has settled. Then Tina got up from the table and took Tony's hand. I lost my footing and like a lioness, I caught up with Tina. Before I could say a word she knocked me senseless, You've got nothing to worry about, Katie. I love children. I'll go on taking care of your daughter. We'll be her family, won't we Tony? Maybe it's best to tell her what's going on. Tony cleared his throat, Exactly, Katie. We wanted to tell you, Tina is pregnant. In six months Sandra will have a little brother.

I hugged Sandra in silence while Tony and Tina were gathering up their things. I don't remember anything else, just a phrase that kept drumming away in my brain that I couldn't suppress, *I'm a grub.* After that, the names of Tony and Tina rang out like hammer blows while I was picking up the coffee cups. I collapsed onto an armchair and it was Sandra who extricated me from my torpor. I'm hungry, Mama. I wished I could have stayed for the rest of my life in the fine, harsh light of this late afternoon. Sandra was insistent, I'm hungry, Mama.

How are your daughters? Léon asked as he finished his massage. Like a nanny, he wiped off every trace of shampoo around my ears. I pretended I was waking up, told him that Sandra and Claire had come for New Year's Day, then I added, hesitantly, They're having a party at noon for my birthday. I don't even know who they've invited.

While he untangled my hair, Léon said, You've landed on your feet. You've survived your second divorce. I didn't let him go on, I want to stop thinking about my exes, Léon dear, no Tony, no René. I want a sexy hairdo, that's all. Léon choked, spilling a little coffee onto his smock, So, Katie, you're in love? The overly direct question left me no choice, Maybe I am Léon. Tonight I'm supposed to be meeting a man I've been exchanging emails with for more than a year and I want to look gorgeous! Léon was tantalized, Have you got a photo? I rummaged in my purse so I could show it to him. Wow! What a dish! This one looks right for you, Katie. How old is he? Fifty? That would be good for you, a younger man. He burst out laughing, And I like his regular features. Another one wasted for men ... Hands off, Léon, make me look like a goddess so he can't resist me.

With all the confidences Léon is told by the men and women who entrust their hair to his scissors, brushes and chemicals, I feel I can trust his judgment. While he finished back-combing my hair, he laid it on a bit thick with the name of my virtual lover, singing to the sound of the dryer, like in *Les Parapluies de Cherbourg, François Rajotte is pampering Katie MacLeod, François Rajotte is a simmering fish, Katie MacLeod is his favourite dish*. Luckily we were alone in the salon.

Are you going to get married for the third time? That's out of the question, Léon, even if ... Unfortunately I hesitated, just long enough for Léon to start up again, Even if, even if ... what, Katie dear? Oh, leave me alone, Léon. I was just thinking about Elizabeth Taylor who was married at least eight times ... Léon adores weddings. I'm fed up with being the old queen, he has often told me. I want to have children, too, like everybody else. It's hard to come to terms with being gay.

I didn't tell Léon that François had proposed marriage in one of his emails. I re-read a thousand times his question, *Would you like to be my bride?* It's insane, I thought. How can he propose to someone he's never met? It may sound crazy, but it's common practice in India, in Africa, where it's parents, not computers who marry off their daughters. I love solitude and I'm quite comfortable on my own, but ever since my father died a little voice has been urging me to *make a new life,* as if my life has come undone along with my marriage. I am moved at the sight of old couples walking around hand-in-hand, Siamese in their thoughts, in their past, in their desires. After fifty, it may become unconditional between two individuals if they've managed to love one another during the period of daggers drawn.

Both my marriages are failures that I've done my best to forget. My memory, like that of an old hard disk, shrank during the autumn and after Papa died indifference gave ground, the ruts became less marked. Léon was finishing my hair in silence and I thought, Comb my hair, Léon, make it fragrant and silky. My hair is my most attractive feature. Take care of it, Léon, convince me that I'm full of beans.

Using the hand mirror that Léon moved around my head, I looked distractedly at my hair. Fluffy, wild, red, cascading to my shoulders. Léon didn't want me to pay him, It's your birthday present! He gave me an appointment for a month later, For your wedding!

I found my big old Mercury which I had to dig out of its snowbank. It was nearly one o'clock when I joined the slow and difficult traffic on Sherbrooke Street. I was annoyed with myself to have come by car. If I'd walked I would have been able to take the pulse of avenue Mont-Royal, breathe a little before I joined my daughters. How had they managed to navigate throughout their childhood among temporary stepmothers and stepfathers? How had they been able to survive? I don't know, perhaps I never wanted to know. Martine and Violette complained that their children lived too close to home, appealing to them for financial, moral, psychological help. My daughters expatriated themselves, a little like Don and Pete. Had I harmed them, given them too much freedom? Sandra often reproached me for separating from Tony, In the beginning, she told me, I preferred to live with Tina and Tony because of my half-brother. You should have worked out a way to hold onto Papa, she added. If he made Tina pregnant it's because you didn't love him enough. I tried in vain to explain to her that life isn't a hundred percent controllable, that love is like blue eyes, the only way to control them is to blind them. When Sandra came to my house she missed Paolo terribly. When Claire was born things sorted themselves out, but how many times did she tell me that Paolo was more fun and nicer than her little sister? She even enjoyed adding, Besides, Mama, Claire isn't my sister. She's the sister of Marlène and Jean-François. And she gets on my nerves! Ever since Sandra got married and no longer lives with me or Tony things have calmed down, but she still sees herself as an only daughter who belongs to a big family in which she is the oldest. As for Claire, she never complained about her childhood. She never criticized me, even if anger and anxiety were hidden in her odd little redhead's shell. She always got out of it through evasive replies and secretiveness, but the day will come when she has to say who she is, what she feels, what she is living through.

Unlike Claire, Sandra always says what's on her mind. Ten years ago, when I told her that I was leaving René, everything came tumbling out, I never liked that René of yours, Mama. He's always watching me. I've always been afraid of him. And Marlène is simply pitiful. Ask her what she thinks of her father, you'll get a surprise. And Jean-François, he's hopeless. Good riddance. Finally we'll all be able to be together, Claire and you and me. Claire was sobbing, You have no right to talk that way about my father. Realizing that she'd made a blunder, Sandra turned towards Claire to console her, embrace her but Claire slapped her, gave her a sharp look with her aquamarine eyes. Sandra's retort arrived, scathing, Marlène isn't your sister, Jean-François isn't your brother, even me, I'm not your sister.

When I left René, I could already glimpse all those tears, but how could I have gone on living with a man who no longer looked at me, no longer saw me, hardly even spoke to me, caught up in his alimony problems, focused on his ex-wife, huddled around his failed marriage? As I was handing René the keys, I took Marlène aside, asked, Are you all right? She hit back, You're cold-blooded, heartless, cruel. You're deserting us. We don't have a mother anymore.

I never saw Marlène and Jean-François again. René was always against it, They aren't your children, he said. Claire spent every other weekend with him for nearly five years, but then she wanted to stay with me full-time. Has something terrible happened? I asked her. Did René touch you where he shouldn't? She burst out laughing. Hardly, Mama, what are you trying to say? It's his ex-wife Brigitte who bothers me, the way she carries on like a worn-out star. She turns up when you least expect her, high heels, manicured nails, purebred poodle. She complains about her piddling alimony and off she goes. Brigitte was still in René's life, she would never leave it, and the breakdown of René's desire for me carried her name.

Along Sherbrooke Street, Christmas decorations shone, powdered with limp snowflakes. Bing Crosby sang "White Christmas" over and over in the tape deck. *I'm dreaming ...* At what moment was mad passion transformed into indifference? How can we recognize the love in films and novels, the love that's supposed to last until death do us part, for better and for worse? Why do we always have to start everything over?

I found a parking space at the corner of Fullum. The snow was falling, heavier than ever. As long as it stops before tonight, I thought to myself. Otherwise the airport will be paralyzed. In the time it took to walk to the house, my hair got soaking wet, a wreck ...

Brunch

AS I WAS opening the door a warm murmur came to me from the living room, then the high-pitched voice of Tony di Sasso clung for a moment to my eardrums. Pudgy, wrinkled, moustached, wearing his perpetual smile, he emerged from the corridor. I hadn't seen him since Sandra's wedding and even wondered if it was actually him: his new coppery brown hair contrasted with the bare head he'd displayed two years earlier. Katie darling, it's been so long, you're gorgeous! He slapped a big wet kiss onto my forehead and the compliments arrived in lip-sync while I was setting my bags down. Is it a toupée? A transplant?

Sandra unbuttoned my coat while she was embracing me just as Claire showed up with a big bunch of mimosas. Here, Mama, they're for you. From Pete. I forgot to say thank you, preoccupied by the choir in the dining room who were singing, *Happy birthday, Katie.* Laid on deliberately so that I'd cry. Who else have you invited, you little witches? Claire tried to calm me down, There's just ten of us, eleven counting you. We tried to have René come, that would've made twelve, an even number, but he begged off at the last moment.

Pete exclaimed, Katie! My sunny little sister! That's my Pete, seductive as ever, you don't let go for a second. I was astounded, as I'd been on my fifteenth birthday when my mother planned a surprise for me in Arntfield, the only time in my life that I'd been the star of a celebration. Don and Pete had been able to bring together all my friends because all the girls had crushes on them. What a party! My father had brought out his violin, the musicians from the Look-Out were there and everyone went down to the store's basement to dance til dawn. It was the first time a boy had put his tongue in my mouth and my ears. The band played "True Love." I remember that, but I can't put a face or a name to that kiss.

Forty years later, Sandra and Claire have brought together our amputated and extended family. At the sight of all those people sitting in my chairs like preserves lined up and displayed on shelves, I thought that time had shrunk. I leaned against the doorframe. Those repeated therapy sessions were in vain, I thought. I'm a limp rag, I'm skidding, dreaming. Behind the cardboard smiles, the haunting voice of Mara Tremblay singing her *Chihuahua, J'me sens comme un chihuahua/Vite sortez-moi de là.* Claire checked my attempt to step back, We really got you this time, didn't we, Mama? Isn't it fun? I said, hesitantly, I don't know if it was such a good idea ...

Claire put her arms around me, and Sandra, who'd stayed in the background, tried to exonerate herself, It was Claire's idea, she's the one who sent out the invitations. Claire led me into the kitchen, It's true, it's my fault. I thought it would be a chance for all of us to be together. You've spoiled us so much. Everyone was thrilled to be part of the surprise. Come on Mama, wipe your eyes. I sniffed, It's the emotion. Sandra immediately prepared for battle, You're always like that, you're never satisfied. Claire felt like seeing her brother and her other sister and I did too. It's your birthday but it's everybody else's party too. Emotion, emotion, you and your emotion. I put myself in her shoes, That's all for today, but don't ever do it again. I whispered in Sandra's ear, You know, I didn't really feel like seeing Tony again. I was about to add, I'm relieved that René isn't here, but Sandra shot her osprey's look at me and I held back.

The conversation started up again, livelier than ever, and I went around the room receiving pecks on the cheek. Pete was on his own for once, without some statuesque beauty at his side. Don was clinging to Sharon, the radiant wife he'd left so often, then come back to *Because of the children.*

Kissing them, I had a kind word for everyone and they replied that they couldn't not be there. George, with a radiant smile, was jubilant at meeting the family. In Salluit, everyone's a relative. Sandra had met George at the Kuujjuaq airport when she was en route to Salluit two years before. Love that struck like lightning, like the love between Gracia and James at the Swastika marshalling yard. She was quickly integrated into the great Inuit family and because George is a bush pilot, she flies around with him from village to village as she likes. They married shortly after they met, it was very important to George. It happened so quickly that no one in our family could attend. I wondered why the big rush. Briefly, I'd thought Sandra was pregnant, but I quickly rejected that old assumption. Sandra explained to me, You know, Mama, whites who go to the Far North to work don't stay long, a year or two, they can't take the cold or the isolation. To make sure that she wouldn't leave like the others, George asked her to marry him. That was in November, 1998, and a few weeks later, at Christmas, when Sandra introduced her George to us, I understood it all. His complexion is smooth and shiny, as if nothing could affect him. He takes care of everything, adores Sandra, loves life. On his cheeks are stretch marks like mine, like my father's, marks that came from his Newfoundland father and maybe from a distant lineage of Scots.

Later, at Easter, I went to see them in their little nest on Hudson Strait. From Montreal to Salluit took more than eight hours, because of all the stops that the Air Inuit plane makes between Kuujjuaq and Salluit, not to mention delays caused by fog. George and Sandra were in the front row of the crowd waiting at the airport, the whole village, or almost, had come to see who the mother of the grade-four teacher was. Inside, the cottage was exactly like our houses in the South. Same microwave, same TV set. Outside, another country. It was minus forty and the snow had no intention of melting. The space was so huge that I felt as if I were floating on another planet, yet I was in Quebec, in my own country, so near and yet so far.

Claire and Silvia were chattering in the kitchen, from where Spanish music was travelling all the way to the living room. They were laughing a lot, but no one understood what they were saying, which pulled George out of his lethargy, Well, girls, so you've come to see us after all? We're coming, we're coming, replied Claire who was in no rush to join the others because she knew that once we were all at the table she would have to translate the slightest word spoken by her friend Silvia, except *Como esta* and *Buenos dias*, which everyone understands.

In one corner of the living room I barely recognized Jean-François in a baseball cap and Marlène, head shaven à la Sinead O'Connor, talking together in a low voice. I don't believe it, I told them. It's been so long, Marlène. I'm glad to see you. And you, Jean-François, you look taller ... Marlène's gaze was more candid, but Jean-François hadn't changed much since the cooking pot had overflowed ten years earlier, when I'd vomited them out of my life.

Marlène, who'd barely spoken to me during all those years when the family was being reconstituted, had learned how to smile, Happy birthday, Katie, happy birthday. I went towards her to kiss her, catching my nose in the ring that she wore in one eyebrow. Jean-François threw his arms around me as if I were still and forever his lifeline. I looked for words that didn't come. Jean-François and Marlène were embarrassed, a little fearful, and in their eyes was the same distress. Sandra intervened, Come on, Mom, we're going to drink to your health. Claire and Silvia poured bubbly into glasses already full. To your health, your good health! I wished I could just take off, go to a movie, go back to Complexe Desjardins and at last see Almodovar's *All About My Mother*, or project my own life onto a screen, shut it inside a strip of film that I'd have placed on a shelf. I did nothing of the kind of course, it would have been a tragedy. I repeated, the better to convince myself, It's over, my name is Katie MacLeod. I like my candy-apple name.

Aware of my uneasiness, Tony said affectionately, Come here, come and sit with your old boyfriend. Over the years my ex had mastered the art of changing the subject, So, Katie, Sandra tells me you've stopped teaching. Lucky you! How do you spend your time now? Do you miss your little monsters? Tony dear, even if I adored my monsters as you call them, I don't miss them. I'm resting. The rest of my life won't be long enough to get over them. With an innocent look, I asked Tony, How's Tina? Without faltering he replied, I've left Tina, and quickly rhymed off his reasons, It got to be unbearable. When Paolo finished his studies, Tina and I were alone and we realized there was no more magic between us. I let him tie himself up in knots. Tony's lies were always more exciting than the truth. When he imagines his life he colours it, turns it into a picaresque novel. He reminds me of my father who, under the influence of scotch, treated us to stories about his childhood and Scotland. It was entertaining, he knew how to keep us spellbound, but finally, all repetition made his stories boring. Tony fascinates me, he talks and talks and I know that eventually he'll come clean. Men like him never change. Excuses are part of their DNA, You know, Katie, it's hard to say this but Tina had changed, she smoked, spent hours and hours at the computer, chatting until late at night. Going through her emails, I discovered that she always chatted with the same man, that he was rich and madly in love with her. I frowned, You dig around in other people's messages? Tony replied, You're hopeless, you'll always be a schoolmistress — like all women for that matter. I wanted to return to the attack, but Pete joined the conversation, You were talking about Tina. What's she up to? We've separated, Tony snapped. You ought to be happy — you, the most hardened and happiest bachelor!

Pete retorted, seriously, that he would have liked to marry too, to live with the same woman for a long time, have children. I asked, Why didn't you think about that sooner? I've always thought about it, Katie, I just haven't met the right one yet.

Don choked on his drink, burst out laughing, Little brother, I can't believe that with all the girls you've gone out with, you've never found a putative mother for your children. Sharon, who'd said practically nothing, put in her two cents worth, Never mind. Don is drunk. You're right, Pete, you should get married and have a child. Don kept it up despite Sharon's worried look, No, buddy, pay no attention to my wife. I think you're fine as you are, brother — no woman, no kids, nobody to explain to. No, really, Pete, if you want my advice, stay as you are. There was an awkward silence. Lips quivering, eyes misty, Sharon got up. The door slammed and Don ran after his wife, apologizing, There she goes again.

Cheeks blazing, Claire and Silvia left the kitchenette to announce with great solemnity, Dinner is served. End of discussion. The gathering hesitated briefly, then everyone came to the table. Claire had brought out everything, the embroidered tablecloth, Grandmother Gracia MacLeod's silverware and china. It's so beautiful, Claire! And my Claire, my creator of warmth, who works wonders with her fingers, looked down, blushing. When Silvia squeezed her hand a thought fluttered in my head, then flew away at once, My daughter is in love with Silvia.

George, sitting at my right, told me in his improved French how glad he was to have come to Montreal for Christmas.

I could hear only bits of his singsong phrases through what the others had to say, they burst out through the hubbub. Katie, Sandra and I are also here to give you some news. At the word *news* my heart skipped three beats. Good news, I hope? Sandra, knowing that the time was right, took a deep breath and stood up, sticking out her belly. I exclaimed, No, no, no, Sandra! It's not true, you aren't pregnant! She threw herself into my arms, Don't yell, please, you'll disturb the baby ...

As soon as she had uttered the word *baby* the conversation stopped. What? What? What's that about a baby? Claire burst out laughing. She already knew, that was obvious. I dissolved in tears yet again, and Sandra told me, reproachfully, Mama, it's your birthday. We did this for you, to make you happy, not make you cry. It couldn't be helped, the dam had burst and I finally broke the silence that had settled in around the table, a long and patient silence, It's so emotional, I can't help it. I never thought for a moment that one day I'd be a grandmother. Sandra suggested a toast to the grandparents. Tony, taken aback by the word *grandparents*, said, No, becoming a grandfather wasn't in my plans. In the general laughter I winked at him and we clinked glasses, Cheers, exchanging a kiss. Tony said, Now I understand why Sandra and Claire invited the uncles and aunts and half-uncles and half-aunts. Sandra blew her father a kiss, Not so loud, Daddy, not so loud. Tony wrapped his arms around her, Congratulations, Sandra my love. That's all he said, but his eyes expressed unconditional tenderness. And I thought, Sandra is loved by her father. What a lead she has in life, lucky her. I don't know if René loves Claire, I don't know if he loves her as much as Tony loves his daughter.

Everyone wanted to pat Sandra's little belly. As it grew the egg would be in the public domain, it would lend itself to cuddles from total strangers as if the mere fact of brushing against a life yet to be born could stimulate, invigorate, rejuvenate. Claire arrived next with a steaming pan of lasagna, saying, It's Sandra's recipe! Then she explained that it was a skilful mixture of her two grandmothers' lasagna. Dear Tony, how he loved Madame di Sasso's lasagna, rich and made from a unique and genuine Calabrian recipe. My mother, who wanted to please Tony, had started making lasagna too, so as not to be outdone, though her Italian cooking had consisted of nothing but spaghetti. With research, labour and inventiveness, she managed to make a lasagna that had won Tony's praise, Your lasagna, Madame MacLeod, is as good as my mother's. Shortly after that, I left Tony, but the hybrid recipe was still alive in the reconstituted families.

Don and Sharon, as red as Christmas balls, went discreetly back to their seats at the table. I told them about the coming of the baby, then the questions began, When are you due, Sandra? Do you have morning sickness? Do you want to know its sex in advance? Will you give birth in Salluit? Sandra stopped the flow of words, It's too soon to talk about that. I'm superstitious. We'll go into the details later. Right now, it's Mama's birthday. A toast to your lovers, Grandma! Everyone laughed and things quieted down after a few mouthfuls. The baby made me forget François Rajotte. Suddenly it seemed ridiculous, that date with a stranger at the very moment when I learned that my daughter was pregnant. If only I'd known.

I'd left the party. Doubts jostled one another, Maybe François isn't at all like his photo or his writing. Maybe he lied to me, maybe his emails had been written by his sister or one of his friends. Sandra whispered to me, You're out of it, Mama. Probably thinking about your date. Then the conversation turned to dating services. I interrupted, Imagine, a good friend of mine arranged to meet a man who'd flown in from very far away ... George looked at me, intrigued, but no one else paid any attention to what I wanted to talk about and the conversation went on, about the advantages and disadvantages of virtual loves.

It was dark, it was snowing hard again and even though it was barely half past two p.m., my apartment, wedged in between two tall buildings, was dim, like a painting by La Tour. The halogen lamp flooded the brightly set table, glasses were refilled, the conversation rolled along. Jean-François and Marlène were baffled by the stories that lovely Silvia, slightly tipsy, told them in a brilliant mix of Anglo-Italo-Germano-Franco-Spanish. Marlène, usually so timid, surprised me, *Me gustan mucho tus historias, Silvia.* She looked my way and smiled. To think that I would have given the entire Earth for just one smile from Marlène when we were all living together in the house in Saint-Léonard.

Marlène moved her chair next to mine, saying in an aside, How's everything, Katie? Everything's fine, Marlène. You? She hesitated, I wanted you to know that I've missed you a lot. I tried to respond, but Marlène went on, No, Katie, let me say what I've been wanting to tell you for a long time. The years we spent with Sandra, Claire and René were the best years of my life. I thought I was going to faint. Come on, Marlène. I haven't finished. I couldn't speak to you because we'd been brainwashed by our mother. She was constantly ranting and raving about you. She called you *the witch*. Your place was ten times more cheerful than my mother's. I admired you …

Tears again. Enough is enough. I ran to the front door, grabbed my parka, pulled on my boots and went out. In the snow, now falling heavily, Claire's voice rang out behind me, The cake! We haven't had dessert, Mama. Why are you running away? You can't just leave like that, we haven't given you your present. I turned around. I just want to get some fresh air. Don't stop the party, I'll be with you again in an hour or two. Enjoy yourselves, I'll be back. I have an appointment with an aesthetician … and then I have to buy a dress. Claire gave up, Whatever you want. We'll be waiting. See you later. I continued on my way and when I turned the corner of Mont-Royal, Claire was still on the balcony.

Poor Claire, I thought to myself as I walked along, she'll have to excuse me, but what a ridiculous idea those daughters of mine had, wanting to bring everyone together, to connect everything — as if we could glue together the thousand shards of a vase that's been broken over the years. I don't have an appointment with the aesthetician, I've only gone once in my life, to have my eyebrows plucked. You have very dry skin, the specialist had said. You'll need a shock treatment otherwise your wrinkles will show up very soon. You need super-powerful creams and you might even consider surgery. No thanks, Madame, we'll talk about surgery and miracle creams some other time, I replied. My ordinary, inexpensive creams do the job. Just pluck my eyebrows, that's all. Will you?

I could have told Claire the truth, simply admit that I couldn't turn back to take another look at the layers of my life. I ran along Mont-Royal, inhaling a powerful dose of exhaust fumes. The entire city had decided to go grocery shopping at the same time, at three p.m. Mont-Royal was buzzing and blowing horns, To hell with my birthday! I told myself as I tried to catch the bus at the corner of De Lorimier, then changed my mind and decided to walk to Saint-Denis.

The Café

I WAS ALREADY breathing more easily. I'd regained control of my life and I held up my head. It's my birthday today, I told myself, and I let myself be taken over by those former lives that were draining all my energy. I have to react, to think that I'll be a grandmother in a few months, la la la, let's try positive thinking. Tony, Jean-François and Marlène seem to be getting used to it. I'm happy about that, but the wound has a tendency to re-open. Everything but Sandra's baby was pulling me down, when I needed momentum to make it to the end of this day, and I thought, I am pregnant with that love as Sandra is with her baby.

Snow was still falling, scattered, slightly wet. It was hard to walk, people going in and out of boutiques that used to be ordinary family-run stores, but now that the Plateau is chic the locals have to find themselves another village. Ten years ago I could speak to my neighbours as I did when I was living with my parents in Arntfield. Then the buildings were sold and yuppies turned them into condos. Grocery stores became fine food emporiums, the bread was artisanal, the greasy spoons, chic cafés. The only thing I'd known about the avenue de Mont-Royal in the '60s was the Mont-Royal Barbecue, where my father and mother had taken me. I'd never seen such extravagance, a restaurant with wall-to-wall carpet on two storeys, like in American movies, where people ate with their fingers, then dipped them in a bowl of water with lemon. Today the building has become a holy credit union.

The snow continued to fall. Léon would have been discouraged at the sight of my wet hair. My daughters, their childhood — it was all coming back to me in gusts: their repeated ear infections, the sleepless nights, their smiles that broke your heart, their fights, their games, their lunch boxes, their ballet and piano lessons. The laundry they brought home from their father's place. An incomparable jumble among days that were as regular as clockwork. And now some good news warms my solar plexus — a baby to be born who might resemble me, or who would resemble Tony or George's parents. Then I thought about my two divorces, exhumed for the duration of a brunch. Tony, René, I wasn't kidding myself, I knew I would always see them through my daughters — in the intonation of their voices, their gestures, their tastes. My life with Tony and René spread out in me like a tide. René still sticks to my skin, a small, hairy caterpillar, unable to speak English, for which James could never forgive him.

René had a knack for getting on my father's nerves when he held forth endlessly without ever lifting a finger. All thumbs, muttered James, incapable of hammering a nail or playing a musical instrument. No, in my father's mind René never measured up to Tony. Even though James had no particular affection for my exes, he did have a weakness for Tony, a businessman like him, Tony the charmer with the voice of Mario Lanza. When we separated, my father was angry with me, not with Tony.

When I met him, René was a single father living with Jean-François, a baby no more than a year old, and Marlène, who was five. He talked to everyone about his separation, which exasperated my father. I wonder what you're doing with that whiner, he said one Christmas night, barely lowering his voice, with no thought for René or for the children, who were present. If his wife kicked him out, with the children, there has to be something behind it.

René told the same story over and over and I still wonder if he'd made it all up. Apparently Brigitte, his ex-wife, suffered from depression, saying that she couldn't see René and the children again, unable to work despite her doctorate in literature. That was before I met René. She changed tack when I told her that he was moving in with me. Unable then to boss around her family from a distance, Brigitte put an extraordinary amount of energy into repatriating her children and her alimony. As she didn't work she had access to legal aid, and how about that? Summonses to appear in court started to drop into my mailbox. But the judge dismissed her case and Jean-François and Marlène stayed with us. Poor Marlène, I can still see her, slim, silent, frightened, picking at her meal, looking down. Once she was in her bedroom I knew that she snacked on old sandwiches brought home from the school cafeteria. She made herself vomit into jars she left lying around in the bathroom.

The situation worsened when Claire was born. Panic. Brigitte started to call non-stop, even at night, threatening to prosecute René again. I begged him not to answer her, but he couldn't help himself, he listened to Brigitte for hours at a time, to contradict her, to threaten her in turn like in a game of psychological wrestling where pleasure collapses into meanness. I began to mistrust René, for whom these rows were his daily bread. With no drama to recount he felt like a nobody and I thought that despite his tremendous intelligence, his kindness, he really was a nobody. More and more he shut himself away in the basement, his complexion grew yellow, his lips white. I was caught in a trap. I knew that I would leave René, but I was chomping at the bit until Claire was old enough to understand.

Jean-François was immediately friends with Claire, more than with Marlène or Sandra. He was barely two years old when she was born and he protected her as if she were his very own baby. In contrast, Marlène lashed out at Sandra, played mean tricks on her, broke her toys, ripped apart her books, and pinched her arms.

Those memories buzzed in my brain while I was walking briskly, head down, weaving between passersby along Mont-Royal. Then, at the corner of Boyer, I straightened up. *Basta*! I want to stop turning over and over those reconstituted, divided lives. Take a deep breath, Katie, look straight ahead, turn and face the future, listen to your shrink who orders you not to take pleasure in your failures.

At the precise moment when I was emerging from my quagmire, who should appear but René. Speak of the devil, I thought to myself. Maybe he won't see me. I fixed my gaze on the juicy grey slush, pretending to be going into a boutique. Katie, this is incredible! I heard. What a coincidence! I thought you'd be at home celebrating your birthday. I feigned surprise, René what are you doing here? It's unbelievable after so many years. I was actually on my way to your place, said René, as uncomfortable as I was. He stammered, When Claire invited me to your birthday brunch, I said no at first. I don't like family gatherings. But then I told myself that after ten years I could make a friendly gesture to please Claire, but I never dreamed I'd see you on the street. Is the brunch over already? I thought I'd arrive in time for coffee or dessert.

Feeling ashamed, I blurted out, I have an appointment at the dressmaker's, I mean at the hairdresser's. I had to leave for an hour or so. Go ahead, René, everyone's there. He hesitated, his foot digging around in the slush, kicking some onto my parka. When I bent down to repair the damage, my head bumped into René's as he was getting ready to do the same. We smiled briefly, not knowing how to keep up the conversation. At least we could have a coffee. I replied, I'm really in a hurry, I have another appointment. Join the others, I'll be home in a while. Go on. René put his hand on my shoulder, something he'd never done when we were together, and I stood there rooted to the spot while he said, You're as beautiful as ever. Even at your age you're radiant. Thank you, René. Don't lay it on too thick. I'll come home after my appointment. René didn't give in, No, Katie, you're the only one I want to see. I want to talk to you. I know, that's hard to believe after everything that happened. You can't say no to a coffee. Afterwards, I'll leave you alone.

I finally gave in. When we stepped inside Porté Disparu, a woman was playing the piano and the image of my mother behind her counter trying to think of a song title came to me. How did she do it? I asked myself out loud in front of René who was silent, preoccupied, aged, worn to a frazzle. He looked at me, intrigued. I was talking about my mother. She knew the titles of every song. Tell me, Katie, what's the title of that one? I think you used to sing it to the children. I replied, It's "Greensleeves." And I thought, Who told that woman to play that tune just as I was going into Porté Disparu?

The café was jam-packed. The pianist played some brilliant harmonies and got up to pass the hat while the tired looking waitress with dishevelled little curls asked if we wanted a menu. No, just a coffee, René hastened to say. Or a beer. Do you want a drink, Katie? The waitress intervened, If you want an alcoholic beverage you have to eat. It's the law.

René gave in, ordered a coffee without taking his eyes off me, as if he was afraid I'd run away. Then he opened the floodgates, Oh yes, Katie, oh yes! These days, especially since Claire arrived, I think about when we were all living together, with Marlène, Jean-François, Sandra. Those were wonderful years. What a family! I wanted to break in, but he tried to move his hand close to mine. I quickly pulled it away. He went on, For years I only saw the bad sides of our life together, what you called a life from hell when we split up. But Jean-François was very happy, he often told me how happy he was. It's true that Marlène was anorexic and she got Sandra into doing drugs, but I don't put all the blame on her. Teenagers all smoke dope or mushrooms and your daughter might have done it in any case. And they stopped. He was hunting for his words. I told him that to get over it all, I'd gone into therapy. Today, I added, I see three of you out of the blue. Marlène, Jean-François and you. As a bonus, Tony di Sasso came to my place. I was sure that I'd exorcised everything, that you were all out of my life, but I realize that I can't erase you all, just as I can't erase my father or my mother even though they're dead and buried. We delude ourselves when we think we have no ties, no affinities with the people we're close to, with our parents, our siblings, our blood relations.

René was out of his depth. He told me, trembling, that he'd had no intention of reviving the old quarrels. What happened, happened. I swear, Katie, I don't want to go back. He looked sincere. I wondered if I was dreaming or if I really was sitting across from him while he chain-smoked. I nearly told him that I was going to be a grandmother but the words were stuck in my throat. It has nothing to do with him, I told myself. Nothing that matters to me matters to him. With a hangdog look René went on, Don't be so negative, Katie. It's true that I wasn't always a lot of fun, that I gave you some rough times but now when I think of the years we spent together, I think they were my best years. No, that's not true, you're starting again, I told René. Stop that right now, it's too much for me. Then he drove his point home, You're the only one I loved, Katie. Sometimes I dream that we'll get back together, start over like we were before.

Sobbing violins. René kept talking, but I could only make out some words here and there that I recall vaguely, Love of my life … I'm sorry … didn't appreciate enough … everything you did for me and the children … Why would he talk to me like that? I asked myself. What's come over him to say that after ten years?

The waitress automatically set the cups of coffee in front of René, whom I'd been observing as if he were an animal in a zoo. His face, his mouth, his cheeks, his eyes had all changed shape. He'd lost the shocks of hair that fell onto his forehead, that he had a habit of scorching with his cigarette when he pushed them back. A few tufts of grey hair emerged, making him look like an accused man admitting his guilt.

All at once I got up, threw my coat over my shoulders and said tonelessly, Okay René. It's nice of you, but it's too late. You've also forgotten great chunks of our life together. Your dependence on Brigitte for instance. How many times did I ask you to finish things with your ex? I have to go. He wanted to keep me there, pushing my cup towards me, At least drink your coffee. You haven't even had a sip, Katie. You aren't going to spend the whole day running away.

Without adding a word I left the café. I wanted to extract the life I'd lived, a nearly extinct volcano that had taken centuries to spew its lava. Standing on the sidewalk, I took a last look at René behind the window of Porté Disparu. I thought, I'm horrible, then I raced to Saint-Denis.

It was still snowing. I could have taken the Metro, drowned myself in The Bay, bought a new dress as planned, but what I needed was to talk to some anonymous person, talk about what had happened to me so as to wash away my past, concentrate on the future, on Sandra's baby, on François Rajotte, on our meeting, our evening, our night. I told myself, Go for it, Katie MacLeod! You're going to fade away if you let yourself go like that. Get over it! The milling crowd on Mont-Royal was making me crazy. I turned onto Pontiac and headed for Saint-Joseph Boulevard. I would breathe easier if I walked past the sleeping duplexes.

François Rajotte, François Rajotte. Repeating his name would make him part of me. His name would quench my thirst. I thought, François writes to me every day. Simply. He doesn't judge me. I don't judge him. Maybe it's easier at a distance. Is it wrong to want to disfigure a virtual love that is so perfect, so satisfying? We could have gone on like that even longer, where does the urgent need come from to see, to hear, to touch one another? I'm walking a tightrope without a safety net. When I see him tonight, I will know if I'm falling. Most likely he'll think I'm ugly. And what will he be like? And the whole family, who'll make a point of being there, will make me trip when I should be free to do as I please?

All that was humming in my head. I was walking, almost running, turning around for fear of being followed by René. The nerve of him! I've made myself vulnerable for the children, so as not to admit to failure. Was I heading for a third failure? I should be able to stop everything, to go home, to think only about my daughters, about the baby, to get older alone and in peace. Why chase rainbows? What do I have to hold onto?

I did hold on, even after Marlène was arrested for possessing and dealing drugs. The police, the youth protection branch — the usual story of a high-risk family: separation, family reconstituted once, twice, a number of children, different fathers and mothers. I was fed up to the teeth and I dropped out on the day I heard a sickly sweet message from Brigitte on our voice mail, Darling, I want you to come back and see me. It was so good last time. We have to talk. We could make a fresh start. It was the same day, but I remember as if it were yesterday, that I kicked René out. Surprised, he wept, swearing that it was a mistake, that he'd made a mistake — in the same breath moaning that he couldn't stand it that Brigitte lived in poverty. He only needed to say, I love you, I can't live without you, but he didn't. It took him ten years to say those words, at the Porté Disparu.

I boarded the 51 bus, which was waiting for me with its door open. With or without a meeting, I decided to go to Laurier Street for a foot-rub.

Feet

I SHOULD HAVE walked and avoided the crowds instead of squeezing inside a packed bus between a pregnant woman with her stroller and an old lady with her bags of groceries. A man kindly gave me his seat. It was the first time in my life that had happened to me and I imagined, Either he thinks I look old or he's hitting on me. I was still mulling it over when he was on his way to the exit.

The day before yesterday, Martine and Violette had given me a gift certificate for a fancy place in Outremont that specialized in the care of feet. The summer before, I'd marvelled at Martine's ruby-coloured toenails at the tips of her sandals. Flattered, my friend had promised that one day she would make a gift to me of a session with her pedicurist. You'll see how wonderful it is. It clears your mind. As the relationship between feet and brain hadn't seemed obvious to me, I'd forgotten about it. When I opened the envelope the other night I thought, The things they come up with, and in the middle of winter! Thanking them lavishly, I stuffed the slip of paper in my purse, sure I wouldn't use it before the summer holidays. At that moment I didn't know that on the very next day, far from sea and sand and sandals, I would be at the door of Beaux Pieds. I smiled. Bo Peep? They may not have any openings, I thought to myself as I climbed the stairs, and came back down. Then I changed my mind, You never know, maybe a cancellation. At the reception desk a monastic silence ruled. All at once a tall, Middle Eastern-looking woman pushed aside a curtain and emerged from behind the shop, a bit of sandwich in her hand. I said, Bonjour, I was wondering if … She didn't let me finish. Yes, Madame, of course, Madame, as you can see there's no one here. Just give me a minute. Get yourself settled, I'll be right back.

When I'd taken off my coat the Middle Eastern woman came back, along with another pedicurist, who was much younger and very blonde. Both were wearing white smocks, like the woman in Holt Renfrew. A nurse's uniform, I thought to myself, a password for the shady zones of sensuality.

With my feet submerged in a basin filled with warm soapy water, I decided to go with the flow, let those good fairies who — as they were rolling my pants up to my knees, before I'd even asked a question — introduced themselves, Djémila and Olga. In chorus, before they began to work, they said, Each of us will do one leg, and they started to massage my calves. They could have gone on forever, as if the words had come out of nowhere, for the sole pleasure of avoiding silence. Where are you from? Who are you? Where are you going? I was in no mood to reply but I made an effort to be friendly. I live in Montreal, but as a child I lived in Arntfield.

Together, Djémila and Olga looked up. Where is that city? Do you know it, Olga? No, Djémila, I don't. I said, It's not a city, it's a little village, population of two hundred, way up north near Rouyn-Noranda. Djémila didn't bat an eyelid. And where is Rouyn-Noranda? I told her, In Abitibi. They didn't dare go further. Then Djémila got the ball rolling, Do you often go back to Abitibi? That's a strange name, isn't it Olga? Yes, Djémila, it must be Armenian. I was about to correct her, It's Amerindian, Madame, but I didn't feel like talking about Arntfield or Abitibi. I wanted to float on the surface, to stay light, stop thinking about my family, concentrate on my relaxed legs. To avoid having to explain anything else, I now asked the questions. Olga, as expected, was from Moscow. And the conversation between my two masseuses started up again as if I weren't there. Djémila had just split up with her husband, with a ten-year-old son to look after. With her ex, it was war. He refused to pay alimony. But she added, reassuring, You see, Olga, how lucky we are in Quebec? They're taking it out of his wages.

Next I found out that thanks to the Internet, she now had a Québécois boyfriend who couldn't stand his ex. Amused, she said, I couldn't care less about my ex, every night my lover cooks my supper, runs me a bath, massages my feet. Can you imagine it, Olga? The masseuse massaged! Olga laughed. So did I. I asked Olga why she had emigrated. Well, you see, Madame, I was so poor in Russia, even though I had a doctor's degree. I earn more as a pedicurist in Quebec than as a doctor in Moscow, it's a miracle, Madame, that I have this job, a miracle. My husband is an engineer and he works as a cleaner for Bombardier. He tells himself that he will be able to work in his field some day. I asked her if they were happy. Olga replied, Yes, but we miss our country and I cry a lot.

Busy as a bee, Olga brought out bottles of nail polish, organized them, put the towels away. She said, I can give you a manicure too for just a little bit more. You can't leave with bare fingernails. I replied, I thought it was included, but I'm tempted to say yes. After all, it's my birthday. Djémila and Olga were hanging on my every word. Your birthday? I echoed her, Yes, it's my birthday, I'm fifty-five today. And guess what: I've just found out that I'm going to be a grandmother. And they were off. That's incredible, you don't look like a grandmother! You're the same age as my mother, said Olga. You should see her, she's really an old lady. Since it's your birthday and since you're going to be a grandmother, we'll give you a free manicure.

Time had passed and I suddenly felt very guilty for having left home so quickly. I changed my mind, No, don't bother. My nails are too short. I cut them as they need it, I bite them out of nerves. Olga stood by her guns. All the more reason to do them, Madame Abitibi, to make them strong, make them pretty, and she filed them, trimmed the cuticles and cut off the bits of skin, what my mother called hangnails, she had such beautiful fingernails, hard and smooth, like mother of pearl. I inherited my father's soft fingernails, defenceless nails that split at the slightest shock. I bring them to my mouth whenever I am anxious. My mother was ashamed of my nails. She would say, You have nails like a man's, you'll never be elegant. I can see her now, filing her nails some mornings before she goes down to the store, dreamy, sipping coffee with a faraway look in her eyes.

Starting when I was born, my mother wanted to leave Arntfield because the mines were being shut down one after another. The Aldermac, the Francoeur, the Wasamac, the Arntfield. When James said to tease her, We're sitting on gold, Don would add very quietly, We're shitting on gold, which infuriated my father. The natives deserted except for some hard core dreamers, who included Ponto Montero, manager of the Look-Out, and James, who ran MacLeod's Music Store. My father, who had never altogether left his mine, gave an Amerindian accent to *Aldermac.* Olga and Djémila would have laughed at the name Aldermac, which didn't sound the least bit Micmac but was formed of a combination of the founders' surnames, Alderson and MacKay, two Torontonians who ran off with all the gold before they closed everything down. James hadn't seen it coming and my mother told him again and again, You see, James, we don't have a taxi anymore or a dry cleaner or a pool room or a bank or a pharmacy. A nightclub, a music store, a small grocery — that doesn't add up to a city. We should leave. The argument started again, my father would say, When the price of gold climbs, we'll be in the right place, we'll be the first to take advantage of it.

During the 1950s, a film was shot in Arntfield called *All the Gold in the World*. My mother had told me, before I went for an audition, With your chewed-up nails they won't pick you. Against all expectations, I landed the role of a tough delinquent who played with fire in the mine shafts. Hélène Loiselle spoke like a Parisian off-camera and sounded like a genuine mother from Arntfield during the filming. I liked everything, the makeup, the costumes, the lines to memorize, the camera, and I swapped my dream of becoming a singer for that of a movie star like Esther Williams. When the filming was over, I confided in my mother, who told me, It's very hard to earn a living as an artist. Actress or singer, it amounts to the same thing. Look at your father, barely scrapes a living with his violin. You are a born teacher. Afterwards, if you're still interested, you could become an actress or whatever you want. Her tone was so convincing that I gave up my dream of Hollywood except on some evenings, in front of the foggy bathroom mirror, when I was combing my long red hair and told myself, Even so, I still have Esther Williams' hair.

When the film came out, my mother admitted, You were good, Katie, but I still don't think it's for you. Then she turned to my father, You see, James, in the film Hélène Loiselle and René Caron decide to leave for Val-d'Or. You buy stock for the store as if the village were going to develop. But this village is dead, understand? My father argued, argued, then he went out, slamming the door. Years passed, I didn't think about Esther Williams again, people fled the village like the villagers in *All the Gold in the World*. James didn't say a word. When the Look-Out burned down for good in June 1972, causing a lot of turmoil, the last grocery store shut down and my father declared bankruptcy. Luckily, with his violin he was able to work in the bars in Rouyn or Kirkland Lake and scrape by. Then he got his government pension and was satisfied with that. My mother kept saying, day after day, We should have left when there was time. We should have left.

Bailiffs came to claim the musical instruments, the cash register, the mikes, and everything else of value. The rest of the merchandise stayed on the shelves — the 45s behind the cash register, the 78s near the display window, the faded scores in alphabetical order next to some plastic harmonicas. My father went downstairs to the store every morning as if he were going to work, gazed at the hit parade list opposite the door, and sat down over some yellowed papers. A few hours later he went back upstairs. We didn't know what he'd actually been doing. There was a good chance that he was slipping into his dream that would never come true; it was a way of activating his past with its gold, its music, and its scotch.

There you go, Madame, I'm nearly finished. Hey, Madame, noted Olga, we told you about us but what about you, have you got a husband? I was too surprised to not reply. I felt myself blush like a little girl, No, I don't have a husband. Olga was insistent, You've never been married? I confessed that I'd been married twice as if I were confessing a sin. And you're all alone at fifty-five! That's horrible! How do you manage? said Olga and Djémila in unison. When I told them that I was just fine without a man, they nearly choked, looking at me as if I'd come from outer space, one putting aside her little brushes, the other holding up her head. Then Djémila lectured me, Look, Madame, you're way too young not to have a man in your life. It's unthinkable. I reassured them, I'm fine, it's all right, don't worry about me.

My two pedicurists bent over again to put the final touches on the last coat of polish, then they blew onto my nails. Olga, intrigued, took up the interrogation, But why are you going to so much trouble to look lovely? Your hands, your feet, your auburn hair, your elegant clothes ... Are you looking for a husband on the sly? You know, nowadays with the Internet, you can meet some interesting people. Come on now, don't let yourself go.

I'd already said too much. It would take too long to explain about meeting François at the airport, about desire mixed with a visceral fear, about the past that kept resurfacing and putting spokes in my wheels. I thought about Sandra's baby, about François, about shutdown Aldermac, the deserted store, the demolished train station, my missed opportunities, about Tony, René, Jean-François, Marlène. It was all being stamped onto my brain, paralyzing me. Too much, it was too much.

Olga and Djémila let the matter drop. Poor lady, don't worry, things will work out. Think about the baby who's going to be born. And look at us, we've found good husbands. So will you, don't lose heart. Olga helped me on with my boots, kindly. It isn't completely dry yet, Madame. I'm going to cover your toes with Vaseline that you can take off tonight. Above all, don't make any abrupt movements. When are you going home? I replied that I was going there now. Olga seemed not to understand. I meant to your own country, to Abitibi. I told her that I didn't go there very often, especially since my father had died. She was pensive while I was giving her my gift certificate. I rushed down the stairs and from the top, Olga called out, Next time you come to Canada don't forget to drop in and see us!

I burst out laughing as I piled into the taxi. Bonsoir, Monsieur, the corner of Fullum and Mont-Royal, please.

The driver tried to talk about the weather, but I didn't respond. Night had fallen, it was nearly half past five, and all at once I felt a need to kiss my daughters. Assuming they're still there, I thought. I wished I could rewind the tape, go back to Sandra's childhood when Tony and Tina were sitting at the kitchen table. The words emerged from my throat, No, Tina, you aren't going to run away with Tony. No, not that. Go away! And you, Tony, stay here with me. I'm your wife. You're Sandra's father. I saw myself letting fly a couple of smacks to his face. Cool down, Katie, I told myself, none of that happened. Tina was pregnant then. She kept her child, she didn't have an abortion. It's like the mine that was closing down, it's still closed even though there are tons of gold underground, even though we're walking on gold. Tony and I loved each other, there was love. True, our love had changed, but it was still there. What to do when someone decides to leave?

And yet when I saw Tony at my table at noon, I felt nothing for him. If he hadn't left with Tina, perhaps our love would have become threadbare because of the children, the bills, the missed opportunities, quick suppers before going to the living room, shoes off, scattered among the papers before we went to bed. Maybe eventually we would have become too tired to hold one another, to kiss on the mouth, with the tongue, to say that we loved one another.

The Cake

BOTH MY DAUGHTERS were alone, a relief! Settled on the living room sofa, watching cartoons on TV. I couldn't stop myself — old maternal reflex — from lecturing them. How can you watch TV so early in the evening? Claire and Sandra jumped, We put the dishes away, we were just taking a break while we waited for you. The others all left ages ago. Mama, why did you run off like that? You didn't even stay for dessert. Why did you pull that stunt on us?

Like a teenager caught falling down on the job, I tried to justify myself. Ah, Christmas, New Year's Eve, the new millennium, my birthday — I think I've had an overdose of parties. Claire didn't let me finish. Yes, but Mama, if we don't celebrate, you're sad, you always criticize us. This year we said, didn't we, Sandra, we were going to pull out all the stops, invite absolutely everybody so that for once you'd be happy. Sandra went further, with a quaver in her voice as if she were going to cry, Yes, we had a fantastic time preparing the brunch, Tony, Jean-François, Marlène, Uncle Don, Uncle Pete, Aunt Sharon — everybody outdid themselves to make you happy.

I was torn between the tremendous pleasure of seeing my daughters, of learning that Sandra was pregnant, and the uneasiness at facing a rush of the past and of amorous failures. My heart was beating so hard that for a moment I thought that I was going to pass out.

Claire came up to me. You're so pale, Mama. We just wanted to celebrate you, that's all. And during the fall you wrote in your emails that you were in fantastic shape, that you'd overcome your past, that Grandpa's death had set you free. I would have liked to tell them that the past was healed and I was cured for good. That was true until I saw Tony, Marlène, Jean-François. I didn't have the guts to admit that I'd run into René on the street, that I'd spoken to him for the first time in ten years and that I was still shaken. The bruise on my heart that was darkening stopped me. After the disastrous brunch, my past resurfaced not through details or anecdotes but like a neglected dog that plays dead, then tackles a child so someone will look after him. I would have liked to talk with them about François, about my date, but all that came out was, Thank you, girls. You did the right thing, but it was too much all at once. I really thought that I'd passed over my past. Claire repeated, laughing, Passed over my past. That's just like you, Mama. You and your word play. Come on, we haven't had the cake, come and blow out your candles, unwrap your presents. I rallied, Yes, you're right, let's wipe out the past.

Sandra and Claire each took me by one arm and led me into the living room, which had become very dark. Snow was still falling, swirling in the window lit by the streetlamp, giving the impression of a warm and empty space. My daughters nourished an impossible dream of cementing the families into one big one, come what may. A family is a father and a mother who stay together forever. After decades of feminism nothing seems to have achieved that desire for "forever," like in novels with happy endings. No, they'll never abandon the sacred tie that I wanted with all my might to get rid of, in order to survive. And here I was with the lasso recapturing me in mid-stampede.

Where did Silvia go? I asked while Claire was setting on the table a variegated raspberry mousse cake with slices of kiwi, peaches, pineapple, and Sandra was opening a bottle of Veuve Cliquot. They looked at one another, To a movie with Jean-François and Marlène. They went to see Almodovar's *All About My Mother*. We stayed behind so we'd have all of our own mother! Guess what, I said, that's exactly the film I want to see! Laughing, we hugged and I added, You're way too generous, sweethearts, champagne, a huge dessert. Bending over, Sandra pushed her hair back, something that I often do. I saw a flash in her velvet eyes, the same one that had won me over in Tony-James-Dean when I met him more than thirty-five years earlier. Sandra is Tony and me, just as Claire combines René and me. Sandra, the dark di Sasso, reasonable like Gracia Michaud, Claire with the flyaway red hair of the MacLeods, Claire the silent Soucy. The cork shot up to the ceiling, Sandra shouted, Papa brought the champagne. And Claire made the mousse herself, thinking we'd be at least twelve at the table.

Before so much cheerful generosity, I felt guilty. I don't know what made me take off like that, girls. Please understand, I just couldn't face all those people at the same time. Sandra froze, Claire nearly burned herself when she was lighting the candles. I was insistent, You're attached to your fathers, that's normal, but I, if I hadn't left those men I would have died, wasted away. Claire replied briskly, You know very well that you wouldn't be dead and you should understand that Sandra and I have brothers and I have a sister … You've got it wrong, Claire, you should say half-brothers, half-sisters. Sandra retorted, I don't distinguish between them and as far as that's concerned I might as well say that Claire is my half-sister because we don't share a father. Life was slipping beneath my feet, like a threadbare carpet; after all those years my daughters were still angry with me for leaving their fathers, that was obvious.

Sandra did not react, but Claire was all aglow. My Claire, so level-headed, confessed for the first time that she'd been relieved when I left her father, that she'd been fed up with our arguments, our moods, the intrusive Brigitte, her stepmother. I should have kept my mouth shut but I said, You see, you don't call Brigitte your mother even though she's the mother of Marlène and François, your "sister" and your "brother." Claire remained speechless and Sandra, who should have kept quiet too, gushed about René, oh yes, René, I could never stand him. And his children were worse. Claire was angry, Come on, Sandra, don't talk about my father, please! I don't know Tony but he must have flaws too. She got up from the table to give Sandra a swat in front of me, and Sandra repaid the favour. Cut it out, girls. Everyone has flaws, including me. Maybe deep down, I thought out loud, I'm meant to be alone, and I'm doing my best to meet someone whatever the cost, and I'm constantly trying to reconcile the irreconcilable, love and liberty when those two words are mutually exclusive. Don't be so glum, Mama, said Claire, embracing her sister. Let's stop talking about the past and please, please, don't start to cry! Come on, let's toast your date tonight, here's to you!

Sandra poured more champagne while the candles were starting to liquefy the raspberry mousse. Make a wish, Mama, make a wish! Let's drink to your grandson or granddaughter, let's drink to the future! Even with three of us blowing out the candles, it was hard to extinguish them all. I wished for the impossible: That my daughters be able to love and at the same time feel free. That the baby will breathe pure air, drink clear water. Sandra and Claire burst out laughing and started to sing, *For she's a jolly good fellow, she's earned her stripes.*

Sandra said, Tell us about your date tonight, this date that's so important we had to turn our dinner party into brunch. Cautiously, I told them about my interest in François Rajotte, what I knew about him from the Open Heart Line on the Internet, the scientific way the agency claims to match up couples. I confessed that I'd checked five hundred items for drawing up my head-to-toe personality profile, starting with my hair colour, my love of music, the family and sex. According to the results, I was eighty-five percent compatible with François, an acceptable rate, according to the Open Heart Line, to guarantee a perfect coupling. Claire asked, Does he speak French? I answered, pronouncing my words and rolling my *r*'s like an Anglo, Not really, his mother is an Anglo from the prairies. Sandra and Claire would have liked me to reveal more, but all at once I felt exhausted and said, I still don't know if I'll go to the airport… It's too late to turn back Mama, you know as well as I do, said Sandra, then she started to hold forth about the science of love that, in her opinion, does not exist. There's no infallible recipe, that would be too easy, she went on, carried away. You pass a test, you get your results, and that's it, you get married with a guarantee, as if marriage is a lawnmower or a car. The mower can slice off your toes if you don't watch out. The car can kill a pedestrian, it can kill you. Everything is so flimsy. Why did you sign up with the agency? Were you that desperate?

The pressure was strong. I didn't have an answer and I gained some time by dipping into my mousse. Ah, the taste of raspberries! How could I forget the rubies gorged with dew that burst open in the summer among horseflies on the shore of Lake Fortune, my mother's jam, her sweet and juicy red pies? Sandra goes on, Take your time, Mama. I asked you a question, you don't have to answer. I emerged from my lethargy, That raspberry mousse is exquisite, Claire, really exquisite. If you go to an agency to find a husband some day, don't forget to say that you make a fabulous raspberry mousse. Claire looked down, got up, coughing slightly, to take her plate to the kitchen. I told Sandra, I'm going to answer your question. I was tired of swimming in the same pond, of meeting the same men who were impossible and available or the same married men who wanted to stay free and not free. At my age ... Sandra tried to protest. I took her hand, squeezed it in mine, Some people say I don't look my age but I know that I'm getting older, my body tells me that every day: a spot here, a white hair there, the sagging skin on my thighs, a lack of energy in mid-afternoon. Though I keep telling myself that I'm full of beans, a voice in my head tells me no: I'm wrinkled, slightly overweight, I lack energy. I have to admit it, I am o-l- ...

Sandra wouldn't let me finish spelling the word, After your hasty departure everyone agreed that you still have your shape. But no one understood why you left so quickly, they wondered if they'd screwed up somehow and I confess they found it hard to believe me when I told them about your appointment with the beautician. Actually I didn't believe you either, but now that you've put Claire and me on the spot, you have to go to the airport, with or without a new dress.

Claire, red-eyed, came back to the dining room carrying a tray with a steaming teapot and china cups from Scotland, mismatched, chipped just enough to show that they're still alive. It was the moment of truth. I said, I didn't go where I said I was going. I went to have a pedicure for no particular reason, because I needed to isolate myself. I even ran into René on the way, I added, with a look at Claire who looked away. Why, Claire, is it so important to you to bring us all together? You know it's not possible, you know that life is over.

Claire stood up. Her red curls fell onto her milky cheeks. Calmly, she gathered up the plates and the champagne flutes, set the cups out on the table, poured the tea. She could have been Vermeer's *Lacemaker*, beautiful and serene in the soft light. I thought about René, who had loved me in a tormented way that didn't suit me, that dispossessed me. I used to be afraid that I wouldn't survive the hostile children who every day, through their silence, reminded me that I wasn't their mother. Claire confessed to me that even though Marlène and Jean-François adored me, they'd said nothing out of solidarity with their mother. What a mess! Everyone was traumatized, starting with Claire, but how can one say anything calmly with that bow permanently taut, ready to shoot at the first thing that moves?

Coming from the kitchen, Claire sat back down at the table. You're right, Mama, it was a volcano, there were too many problems, no one could breathe in the house. Our family, reconstituted and then dismembered, had become so volatile, so enigmatic that it no longer had any purpose. Sandra had left her raspberry mousse on the table and it was spreading across the white plate, it could have been a pool of blood. Come on, Sandra, don't be like that. Say something, have a bite to eat. Sandra dropped her fork, You've already forgotten that I'm pregnant. I'm nauseated, that's all, it's normal. You must have been nauseated too, don't you remember?

I restrained myself to keep from answering her reproach and went to my room, leaving my daughters over their cups of tea. Sandra cried, You always say that poor Claire had two families but me, even though I've lived in four different families, I don't feel like a victim. It's true, I thought, she lived with Tony and me, then with Tony, Tina and Paolo, then with René, Claire, Marlène, Jean-François and me, then with Claire and me, then sometimes with René, Claire, Marlène and Jean-François without me. It could drive you crazy. If my count is accurate that makes five families. Sandra joined me in my room, the way she used to do when she was little. Sandra, the searcher in drawers, always wanted to know everything, most of all not miss anything. She called her sister while she was opening my closet, Come here, Claire, we're going to pick a dress that our future-ex-stepfather will like. Looking contrite, Sandra added, I couldn't either, I couldn't take any more of that never-ending pandemonium. The years when the three of us were together, Claire, you and me, were the best. We were all healthy, we breathed, we laughed, life was light. And now I'm at Tony's with George and we're very comfortable. I've been doing better without Tina around but I miss Paolo a lot, you can't imagine, you don't know my little brother.

Claire went at it again, Aren't you discouraged, Sandra? You want to have a child anyway? Not me, no way. Sandra went through my dresses one by one, then she laid a black shantung on the bed. You should wear this one, Mama. It's classic, you'll look wonderful in it. Claire added, Don't forget the pearls. Basic black with pearls, a winning combination. Then Sandra spoke to Claire, I want this child with all my heart and I want to give it a better life than mine, than Mama's, than Grandmother Gracia's. Then Claire noticed my feet with Vaseline on my toes. Oh Mama, she said, your red nails are sexy. I didn't know if I should laugh, but the girls burst into giggles and Sandra added, sardonically, while she put her arms around me, Don't worry, Mama, Claire and I often say that we'd like to be as beautiful as you are when we're old.

I put on the black dress without telling my daughters that it was the one I'd worn to James's funeral. I added, Sandra, I think that the only reason to have a child is to forge a life from what's left of our own. I spent my whole childhood in the same ghost village with the same frustrated parents. Was that any better? I can't escape the burden of my father, his anger, my mother's chronic anxiety, her insidious suffering that leaked out with every move she made, every word she spoke. I didn't learn to be carefree, that was why, after a while, I broke up with René. I left because I needed air, because I wanted to sleep alone, to think alone, to eat alone. Otherwise I'd have gone off the rails. Anyway, girls, this is turning into a melodrama, let's pour ourselves some champagne.

I took Sandra's plate, threw out the rest of the crushed raspberries, winter raspberries from California that have nothing to do with the raspberries from Lac Fortune.

The Gift

CLAIRE AND SANDRA ordered me to hold my breath. We've got a surprise for you! Another one? I said, incredulous and a little panicky. The two girls rummaged in a big bag. Light muffled laughter, as when they were children and wanted to cover up some naughty behaviour. Then, with her hands behind her back, Claire said, as she slowly extricated an envelope, Here, Mama, it's from the two of us and your brothers. My brothers? I hurried to pierce the mystery, but Sandra intercepted me at once, We're going to play Academy Awards. Finalists for Best Actress in a Supporting Role are: Katie and Mama. And the winner is, the winner is — Mama!

Claire cleared her throat: For your birthday Sandra and I decided to give you verbal flowers and since flowers never come without a pot, we'll start by giving you the pot. When I was in grade two and we went to the school where you taught, we were ashamed of you. You didn't look like a teacher, you wore jeans, your hair was scruffy, you were never on time. We would have liked a mother like everybody else's, the ones who waited for their children in an apron, the table set, a mouth-watering aroma of soup on the stove. You didn't want us to take classes in religion or to make our first communion. Luckily we didn't have the same name, yours was MacLeod, mine was Soucy and Sandra's was di Sasso. We didn't have to admit that you were our mother, which was fine with us. We could put up with some clouds for another half-hour. Couldn't we, Sandra?

Never would I have dared to say a thing like that to my mother. If I insulted Gracia now and then when I was in my teens, I'd been stagnating in Arntfield, where the only place that attracted me, the Look-Out, was forbidden. At fifteen, one very hot night when the sun was disappearing in its chariot of fire, I'd edged my way through the fire escape towards the Look-Out, hobbling along in my mother's high heels, wearing an emerald green tussah silk dress that I'd made for myself on the sly, a flowing dress that only covered my torso, from armpits to crotch. At the back of the room packed with dancers swaying their hips to a diabolical rock 'n' roll, James was at the bar, talking with a woman in makeup and sequins. I was dancing not far from the door and as soon as a set had finished I raced outside, covered in sweat. I made it go on with nobody the wiser until the wee hours and just as I was about to leave,

I came face to face with my father, who was clinging to the arm of his starlet. Until yesterday I'd held back the painful wave of that encounter, but when Claire said, We didn't have to admit that you were our mother, which was fine with us, everything came back in the slightest detail. I felt James's hand grab hold of my hair, my cries followed the railway track all the way to Kekeko, then came back to me like a breaking wave of pain. I barely listened to Claire who was partway through her pompous speech, Dear Mama, after the clouds, here comes the sun that Sandra has brought you. I lost my composure, on the brink of tears again. Claire wrapped her arms around me. It was a joke, Mama. The rest is wonderful, you'll see. Your turn, Sandra!

Sandra stood up. Yes, we'd have liked to have a family home, like you had in Arntfield, to have the same father, the same mother all our lives, not have to pack our bags every weekend — that, we couldn't hide from you. But there is one thing we're proud of, which is that you never deviate from your beliefs, your loves, your desires. And today not only are we not ashamed of you but we envy you for surviving ... Stop, Sandra, There's too much sun, I'm choking!

Sandra and Claire kept it up, but I ordered them to stop the farce. What a day, what a never-ending birthday! That will teach me to want a celebration, that'll teach me! Open your present at least! said Sandra, handing me the envelope that had become damp in her hands. I had trouble opening it.

Oh là là! a plane ticket. Destination, Aberdeen. All inclusive — hotel, car rental for two weeks. Dates to be confirmed. You're absolutely crazy, who told you that I wanted to go to Aberdeen? From the way they looked at me I realized that my question was pointless. I've always carried on about how much I want to go to Scotland. I could have paid for the trip with my inheritance, but I didn't want to keep the money that James had accumulated by depriving himself and my mother of legitimate treats. When I criticized him for putting aside too much he replied, You never know, I don't want to be obliged to sponge off you. Until the end he spared no expense for just one thing: his beloved automobile, the Mercury that he'd left to me. He had paid cash for it and the salesman had been intrigued by the old man in a too-small jacket who was haggling over a boat-sized car.

I didn't know what to think about the gift, a Greek-type one perhaps, that would plunge me into an even more distant past that would drain the small amount of energy I still had, that would stop me from facing serenely the countdown of my life. Fifty-five years old today, in ten years sixty-five, in twenty years seventy-five. I don't dare look any further ahead, I refuse to see myself at eighty-five, the age my parents were when they died.

Claire whispered in my ear, There's one thing we forgot to tell you: Sandra and I may be able to join you. I protested, Sandra's pregnant and Mexico is a long way from Scotland, but Sandra went on, The doctor told me that if all goes well, it would be fine for me to go to Scotland next spring and Claire thinks that her university will still be on strike, that she won't go back to Mexico.

I didn't know if I should be glad. The trip that I'd never imagined taking other than alone, combing the streets to look for my paternal grandparents' house, my cousins, to feel the North Sea air, to gaze out at the cemetery of the sky that shelters other MacLeods as red-haired and wild as I am.

Faced with my lukewarm reaction, the girls were thrown off balance and, stammering, they picked up the thread of the conversation. My head felt ready to burst. The gift was rekindling a fire that was smouldering, violent. Droning, Is it possible that my daughters are as angry with me as I was with my father? Am I a burden for them? They're upset with me, they told me, I know it, but they don't dare go any further, to spare me, the way I spared my mother, the way my mother spared my father, secrets after secrets, to the point of suffocation, the loss of memory, everlasting before death.

I finally got my wits back. Sandra was trying to change the subject by talking about her imminent departure for Salluit, Maybe you'll be there when the baby is born, Mama, in August. I'm going to organize things so I'll give birth in Kuujjuaq and I'd like you to be there. Oh là là! Sandra, two big trips the same year! I'm out of breath just thinking about it.

My daughters went on with their conversation, but I was listening abstractedly, deep in thought. My parents are dead, Sandra's going to give birth, that's the order of things, I thought to myself. My mother wasn't with me when I gave birth and I wonder if I'll be able to be with Sandra when her baby comes into the world. Why shouldn't we do those normal things that all mothers do? I would have liked my mother to be home at noon when we came home from school, that she'd bake a cake every year for my birthday. She was behind the counter waiting for customers. And my father wouldn't have lifted a finger to make a single meal. Mother and cook on the verge of being a grandmother, I no longer have the courage to make even one family meal. What kind of grandmother will I be?

Sandra and Claire were chattering away and suddenly the name *Silvia* emerged, along with the phrase *in love*. I emerged from my lethargy, asked Claire to repeat what she'd said, I didn't quite get it, I said. No, Claire told me, you understood perfectly well. Silvia and I are together. I thought you'd figured it out. I didn't want to tell you in front of everybody.

I staggered under the blow, as we do when a disease long suspected is finally diagnosed. I said, Silvia's very nice and all I want is for you to be happy. Claire imitated curtly my tone of voice, All I want is for you to be happy. You didn't say that when Sandra married George ...

I took my time, sat down next to Claire and Sandra,

collected my thoughts and tried to find the appropriate words. I felt that I was stepping onto dangerous ground. That's not true, Claire, that I disapprove. In fact I don't have to approve, it's your life. I'm still surprised and I'm not sure what to say, that's all. It isn't every day that a mother learns that her daughter is in love with another girl. Whether I want it or not, I feel guilty. Guilty of what? Claire asked. I replied without thinking, I don't know, guilty of not giving you a positive image of men. What did I do? Nothing, Mama, nothing. Ever since I was a little girl, I only desired women, that's how it is. It's like blue eyes, as you often say, there's nothing we can do about it.

The questions jostled one another in my head. How did that desire express itself? At what age? What did I fail to do in her education? Then Claire tried to give a better explanation, I love Silvia, Mama, there's no doubt about it, but what makes me happy is to have told you. And I'll be even happier on the day when you accept me as I am.

So all I could add, Claire dear, was, *I'll do my best to understand*. Every one of my words startled my daughter and made the dishes clatter. I saw from the back my daughter who's so beautiful, a redhead like me, and I thought that she wouldn't have children. It's weird, before today I never imagined that I'd be a grandmother, now here I am missing the grandchildren Claire won't give me. I have friends who are lesbian, but that my own daughter could be homosexual never crossed my mind. A glass broke in the sink, Claire exclaimed, Shit! and I was able to say calmly, Why are you so upset, Claire? I'm not judging you, I'm just telling you that I'm surprised. As you must have been when you realized that you loved a woman. Claire agreed, admitting that it hadn't been easy, that she'd felt alone before she dared to take the plunge. Being somewhere else, in a foreign country, helped me make the leap, she admitted, and now that everyone knows, let me say it again, I'm relieved. She glanced with boundless affection at Sandra, who approached. I took them in my arms. My little girls, my little girls. Then I thought that if such a thing had happened to me I'd never have had the courage to admit it to my mother, even less to my father.

I was so tired, as the day advanced I got in deeper and deeper. I'd have given my soul to have my freedom restored, my wonderful solitude, to refocus, lighten myself. There was a grain of sand in my mouth and the plane ticket on the table among the china cups now seemed frivolous. Both my daughters were there, it was my birthday, the beginning of a new millennium, I was supposed to meet my Winnipeg lover in a few hours, everything should have been for the best in the best of all possible worlds. The heaviness in my chest, the silence interposed between my daughters and me — all of it clipped my wings.

Night had really fallen, we couldn't see a thing outside, but a lamp shed light on the piles of plates and cutlery on the counter waiting to be washed, the bottles lined up next to the garbage can like so many empty words. Would the plane land in spite of the snow, in spite of the fog? I wondered suddenly. The flight would have to be put off til tomorrow, til next week, when Sandra and George will be in Nunavik, when Claire and her lover will have found an apartment, til Marlène, Jean-François, René and Tony will be back in their own places in my distant memory. I would like to have no more ties, to take a deep breath, lower my shoulders, unlock my neck.

Sandra read the panic in my eyes. She got up, gently moved my head to her belly, Mama, don't worry. We love you, that's why we give you a hard time. Claire and Silvia don't need us to help them love one another. I hit back and said, carefully weighing my words, I can't take any more, girls, I'm sick of being in the dock. You have a big day tomorrow and I want to get ready for my date. On her way to the door Sandra added, You hardly told us anything about this François, our third father. I followed her into the hallway shouting, Don't expect anything from me! I'm definitely not getting married again. Sandra grabbed her coat, So you say, so you say.

While Sandra and Claire were getting dressed, I told them about some amusing emails from François. He has a sixteen-year-old daughter called France, I added. Claire wanted to see a photo of her future sister, she said. Sandra corrected her, Quarter-sister, you mean. Claire burst out laughing, Quarter of a chicken, you mean. And I, who didn't have a photo of France, laughed at her tinkling laughter. When they left the apartment the snow was falling harder and harder and they cleared a big limousine that looked vaguely like my Mercury. Who owns this ocean liner? I asked. Oh come on, it's Tony's. You ought to know, Sandra replied. He couldn't stand it that your car was bigger and more luxurious than his. Oh, hang on a second, Mama, I forgot. Sandra rummaged in her backpack and presented me with a package tied with a ribbon. Uncle Pete gave me something for you. It's letters from Grandma Gracia.

While the car zoomed off, I waved to my daughters who didn't turn around. Barefoot in the snow under the balcony.

The Letters

BACK HOME I wiped my snow-covered feet, gazing at my ruby-red nails. I needed urgently to rest my mind after so much hullabaloo. An earthquake, an eruption, lava from the past, I told myself, there will never be enough volcanoes to expurgate myself. I put Pete's letters on the table and before sitting down I poured myself a big glass of water, wondering if it wouldn't be wiser to wait for the dust to settle. Smoke and gas and lapilli, as I used to tell my students. I liked to teach them the precise words, the rare words, and I imagined that the children would be very proud and enjoy telling their parents, Today we studied volcanoes and smoke and gas and lapilli. You know, the kinds of gas and the little stones the crater spits out ...

The package of letters was pleading, Open me. I resisted briefly, telling myself that I couldn't waste any more time.

It was nearly seven o'clock, the plane was due to land at eight-thirty. I had to leave by seven-thirty at the latest. Barely an hour to get ready. Just imagine, I thought that when I was no longer teaching I'd have all sorts of spare time and be able to relax when I wanted. An alarm clock in my body always goes off early like a pacemaker that's been inserted without permission. I feel a twinge. I wonder if I've prepared my class, if little Jacob or Marie-Sol will be ready. Then I realize that it's a nightmare and that I'm giving myself advice. No, Katie, calm down, you don't have to go to school, there's no Jacob or Marie-Sol in your life now. That's over, all over. You have no more commitments. Every idle moment becomes a gem of destiny. You have no more schedule, you have all the time in the world — time for yourself that you've never had, always swept up in the whirlwind of things to do, of shopping lists, meetings, turning in grades, meetings with parents. Now that you've ejected yourself from the maelstrom, now that you aspire to have no more plans or even desires, to live in a kind of nirvana, not to give a damn about anything — money, love. To be a convalescent for the rest of your life.

Now I've let myself in for a new set of problems, I thought, organizing my time so I won't be late for a romantic date. Why is life always against the current of my decisions? I don't want to retrace my steps and I'm dying to read that bundle of old letters; that's all I want. I did a quick calculation: I had half an hour. I gave in to temptation, frantically untying the red ribbon around the envelopes, yellowed like the petals of a withered daisy, Gracia's letters were spread across the table in a circle. One, addressed long ago to Pete, was written with confidence. On another, which most likely dated from the time my mother spent in the institution, the handwriting was jerky, broken, nearly illegible. The envelope, addressed to James, was unstamped and still sealed. As I opened it, I wondered why this letter had ended up with Pete's belongings. Probably my father had given it to him without noticing that it hadn't been mailed — or would Gracia have accidentally put it inside a letter sent to Pete? On the crisscrossed lines the words overlapped, words exhausted by pain, *James, I lov yo but friends never, jamie, i jamie, I james you, xxxx, whyyyy, wehhy, weeehhy, www.* Her handwriting deteriorated as she did. So very sad, she who used to write so well, whose thinking was so straightforward, who loved words. It's inconceivable. Then I took another letter, older, this one, very thick, dated 1982. The writing was smooth, delicate, slanted slightly left. *Dearest Pete, You'll find a cheque for five thousand dollars as we agreed on the phone the other day. Please be discreet with your father, Don and Katie. You have to promise me to keep the source of this money secret. No one knows and the secret must be kept that I know who started the fire at the Look-Out ten years ago. It was June 12, 1972, the night was clear and warm. I wasn't asleep and I decided to go out and walk down rue Principale. All of a sudden I saw the husband of Judith, our dear countess, come hurtling down the Look-Out hill. He wasn't expecting to meet me along his way and barely said hello. Looking up, I saw big flames shooting into the sky. I said to myself, Oh my, the Look-Out is on fire. I turned around and when I got home I didn't call the firemen. I got back into bed, relieved, thinking that Judith's husband had been brave enough to do what I'd wanted so badly to do: set fire to the love nest and put an end to my humiliation. The next day, Judith was accused of arson and that same night I got a call from her husband, I know that you saw me last night, but I'm ready to buy your silence. I couldn't stand seeing them together at the Look-Out every night. The same for you, I imagine ... I accepted his offer and I have no remorse for having taken those ten thousand dollars. The guilty party was not me. Before departing for the United States and leaving Judith for good, after making sure that appearances incriminated his wife, he gave me the money, saying, At least those two won't have a place to meet. I kept it hidden for ten years in case someone found out what had been going on. I'll give Don the other five thousand but I won't send anything to Katie because in any case, she couldn't care less about money, she seems to have a problem with business. She was here this week, pressed for time as usual, but she's helping out. I would like her to move back, it would be easier for your father and me. Ever since the store closed I've been feeling useless. I want to move to Montreal, but James won't hear of it. He still thinks that the price of gold will go back up, that the village will come back to life. I won't change him, he's been deluding himself since he first set foot in Arntfield. The village will never come back to life, the region will die a natural death once the mining companies have extracted all the ore, cut down all the trees, polluted all the lakes. Then we will be forced to leave. Or die of boredom. Dear Pete, I have no one to talk to, I wish so much that you would come to see us more often. I know that your father doesn't approve of your lifestyle but I'm sure that deep down he's proud of you. Now that I'm old and can't do anything but the dishes and a little housework, I have time to think about your childhood which I hardly saw, hardly appreciated. It was Katie who brought up you and Don, finally, but what choice did I have? I had a gun to my head. I see again certain moments, trivial little flashes. For instance when we all sang "Greensleeves" together on the stage at the Look-Out. You were already a fine musician. James has his failings but he's a fine musician too. He may not have given you a lot of love but he did give you music, which is love. Your loving mother, Gracia.*

I felt at once betrayed and relieved. The Judith my mother talked about at the end of her life, the Judith my father claimed not to know. Don was in on it too, but why had my brothers never mentioned it to me? It's true that I don't talk to Don very often — and that Pete is far away. My mother had some moments of lucidity and I understood better now an odd story she'd told me shortly before she died, a story so weird that I'd attributed it to dementia. She'd said, I was sleeping in your room. I often sleep there, Katie, since you left, because your father reeks of alcohol. The other night, in the middle of the night, I decided to go and join James. When I moved the covers, there were two of them in the bed. I recognized Judith. The nerve of her, sleeping in my bed, in my house, with my husband! I turned around and went back to your room and the next morning, when I mentioned it to your father, he told me I was crazy. It was just a bunch of covers, he said, but I was sure that his Judith was in my place in my bed.

I tried to calm Gracia, Don't think about that, Mama, stop thinking about it. The nurses at the clinic had advised me not to go against her, to go along with even her zaniest stories, use diplomacy to bring her back to reality. So I reassured her, That happened so long ago, Mama. Don't think about those old love stories. My mother answered, No, Katie, it's not all that long ago. He still sees her. I know that he brings her here when he thinks I'm asleep. I hear them.

I hadn't believed a word my mother said. I'd told myself that her condition was more serious than I'd thought, but the anecdote kept bothering me and I tried to talk to my father about it just before he died. He stopped me, shrugging his shoulders, his eyes sad, Come on now, Katie, that was her disease, forget it.

It was twenty past seven. I had to leave for the airport if I wanted not to miss François, but I decided to have one last glass of champagne. I went back to my room to put on my pearls. Basic black with pearls, Claire had said. If I wear this mourning dress, I told myself, it will be as if my father is coming with me to my date. I opened my closet and quickly took off my black dress, donning a flowing blouse and my pale grey skirt, the one that swirls around my legs and makes waves. The skirt resembles the one that Pauline Julien wore in the scene from the film *Bulldozer* that was shot in the rundown hall of the Look-Out. My mother adored Pauline Julien and she had offered her services as an extra. That was in April, 1971. I've never forgotten. I'd come to Arntfield to give Gracia a hand with the store inventory because she was considering selling. James resisted, went on strike. For him, closing this store, deserted by its customers, was out of the question, this store that hadn't brought in a penny for years, that was piling up deficit after deficit. We're going bankrupt, she said. I should have gone on teaching instead of working for your father. I tried to cheer her up as much as I could, but it was a waste of time until the film *Bulldozer* came and disrupted our lives. James was annoyed because the filming kept him from going to the Look-Out for his scotch every night, in the company of the Countess of Farmborough. I took my mother to the main hall when Pauline Julien, standing on a table, sang to an audience of rowdies. Then I remembered our family performance, bringing back to my heart "Greensleeves" and the desire I'd toyed with to become a singer. After the song, during the intermission, Pauline Julien met with my mother and me, kindly but no more than that. What beautiful hair! my mother said. Flaming red like yours, Katie, and it's true that with hair like yours you could have become a singer. Come on, Mama, I replied, you don't sing with your hair! No, said Gracia, but it helps. Pauline Julien's voice isn't outstanding and she's sometimes off-key, but her hair is fiery, she's high-spirited, hot-blooded, she has on a lovely grey skirt that falls over her body like a cloud. That's all important. You have the hair but not the spirit. I didn't let her go on. I snapped, All right, Mama, I get it.

In my mother's mind, my case had been dealt with long before. I was twenty-six, married, I taught elementary school, there was no other possibility in my life. There was always something I lacked to be successful, to make my dreams come true. What is the significance of hair and figure and a voice without spirit if you're not fiery, determined? I am a married woman who teaches. That sentence in the present indicative had moved indiscernibly from the mother's head into the daughter's. That's the way it was, indisputable and eternal, inscribed in the daughter's trust in her mother.

Gulping the glass of champagne on my bedside table, I thought that my mother must have been hurt when I didn't believe her about Judith. In my Pauline Julien outfit,

I thought to myself as I looked in the mirror of the wardrobe, I really do look like a singer. I fluffed my hair with my fingertips. *Non, rien de rien, non, je ne regrette rien, la la la la la,* and I headed for the bathroom to cover up my fine lines and my age spots. The truth leapt to my eyes and I stopped short. I should have gone to the a esthetician. There are bags under my eyes. One of these days I should have these ridiculous fine lines and spots removed, but I'm afraid of the knife and of botox and its friends. Too chicken to make myself look younger, that's how I feel. I touched up my makeup, applied lipstick with a finger, the way my mother did and dropped a red kiss on the mirror of the medicine chest. I sang under my breath, *Grandma do you want to dance, Grandpa would you like to waltz,* and I quickly downed another glass of champagne as I went into the kitchen. In any event, I thought to myself, I'll take a taxi to the airport. If I go ...

On the low table in the living room old photo albums sat next to overflowing ashtrays. Tony must have asked to see the photos, I thought as I picked up the most brittle album. The photos of Sandra as a chubby little girl flanked by her parents. Tony and me, the model couple just before the marriage collapsed. Sandra in Arntfield with her MacLeod grandparents. Gracia looking drawn, at loose ends, tired, in her usual white blouse. James with his lively expression, looking elsewhere as if he'd seen an apparition. Sandra, who looks about five years old, meaning that James was sixty and Gracia fifty-five. My age. She looks like a lost old woman, maybe she was in the early stage of the disease. She spent the rest of her life just surviving, telling herself again and again that she should have left Papa when they shut down the store. Why did she stay on, keep turning over her boredom, waiting for her husband to come home tipsy from his escapades with that Judith? As I turned the pages of the album I heard my mother close by whispering in my ear, I'm going to leave James, leave Arntfield, travel, visit my children. I thought, She never dared to do that, she let her mind go in circles with her little habits, let helplessness submerge her. Poor Gracia. James was able to escape because he had enough imagination, with the help of alcohol, to create friends, adventures, harebrained ideas for himself. He looked elsewhere, as we saw him do in the photos. Until the end, he looked like a gangling teenager with his tousled hair and his baggy pants. On the last page of the album a moving photo of René, smiling, flanked by Marlène, Jean-François and Claire. It was just before the break-up, before I kicked them out, him and his children. Only afterwards did I discover in the basement, when I was cleaning it, an unidentified videotape with strange black stripes. I fed it into the drive and the first images were of a young girl, naked and with hands and feet bound. She was crouching in a kind of grotto filled with candles and suddenly a man appeared out of nowhere to insert a lit candle into her. I nearly fainted but a kind of morbid curiosity made me press the fast forward button, then I saw another sequence that showed the young girl dying while her torturer was ejaculating. I was stunned by the discovery and I buried that secret inside me for years before entrusting it to a psychiatrist. It's completely normal, he told me, for a man to use such methods when his wife is frigid. I'm not frigid, I protested, and I walked out and slammed the door. Later, I read in the paper that my psychiatrist and his frigid woman had been arrested for pedophilia. I removed the photo from the album and tore it into shreds. Why had I forgotten all that when I ran into René at Porté Disparu this afternoon? I haven't got a memory, I only thought about Brigitte, Brigitte, like a scapegoat.

I closed the album and called a taxi.

The Taxi

I PICKED UP my plane ticket gift, stuffed it in my purse, then put on my black coat. First though I wound my blue-and-green tartan scarf around my neck so François would recognize me, but at the last minute I took off my coat and scarf and put on my parka. Just in case. I pulled my long red hair behind my head and repeated out loud, the better to convince myself, My name is Katie MacLeod and I spit fire. I went outside to wait for the taxi. I didn't trust myself, I was afraid I'd change my mind. It had started snowing again, yellow and white, under the streetlamps. Farther away, the avenue du Mont-Royal was quiet now, the store windows scarcely lit up. My watch read a quarter to eight. Let's hope that there won't be too much traffic on the Metropolitan highway, I thought. I should have been totally delirious, thrilled at the prospect of meeting a man who desires me, who wrote love letters to me, who travelled from Winnipeg specially for me — but I kept clinging to my confusion, wondering why I was there, outside, wanting and not wanting to go to the airport. Then I thought better of it, Come on, Katie. He won't recognize you. You aren't in your black coat or your blue-and-green scarf. The ball is in your court. I can take off if he doesn't appeal to me, I've got nothing to lose.

A gentle wind barely scattered the light snow. I'd have liked to walk along the street that way all evening, not have to make a decision, to wander, to feel new and without a past. While I was pacing outside the house, questions were muddled together in my head, Why turn my life upside down? What about these years that are piling up, that I carry like an overloaded backpack? Am I about to make another mess?

Through the lace curtain on my living room window my plants and books offered me peace. How can I live and have peace, how can I love and have peace? All those conflicting matters call for life against death, death against life. I had almost decided to go inside, to drop everything, when I saw the taxi turn onto Fullum Street. I piled in like a robot. The airport, please. Dorval or Mirabel? No baggage? No, monsieur.

To show that he'd got the message, the driver tuned the radio to a marshmallow music station. He wouldn't say another word during the entire trip, you could tell, which suited me fine. I'd have liked to go inside myself, but the image of René's video, still clear in my memory, came back again, unbearable. I must stop thinking about it. I must think instead about the baby who is going to be born, about the raspberry mousse, about the ticket to Scotland in my purse, about "Greensleeves," my father, my mother and my brothers onstage at the Look-Out, about Sandra, so pretty with her black curls, about Claire, clinging to me, sucking so hard on my heavy breasts, about my snot-nosed pupils the day before Christmas holidays who gave me a kiss, about ... No, I can't help it, that pornographic image came back to me like a hallucination. How had I been able to live with that stranger beside me, with whom I'd made love, that stranger who could come while he watched a woman die? That ordinary man who gave me my little red-haired Claire, who worked to earn his living? How is it possible? There are no guarantees. But why me? Am I as frigid as my dubious psychiatrist next door to Holt Renfrew claimed? After every session I felt an irrepressible need to spend money, even if it was just ten dollars for some cut-rate trinket, to console myself, to forget for two seconds that I was the most frigid bitch on earth.

An accident at Décarie created a colossal traffic jam. Snowflakes were falling in slow motion, as in a snow globe of Niagara Falls. We stopped long enough for me to change my mind one more time. I was absolutely positive that it was better to turn around and go back, not go to meet

François. I wanted to shout, Monsieur, I want to go back to Fullum Street, I don't want to go to the airport, but as in a dream the shout stayed in my throat, frozen, and I didn't say anything, most likely stuck with my urge to do the opposite of what I wanted, yet again. I thought, Is it possible for an unspoken desire to be stronger than any reasoning? You're horny, Katie MacLeod, you need to have a man in your bed every night, to hear him breathing at your side when you wake up, to prepare meals for two, for all that to drown your will, what you are, your lifeblood. Then immediately I felt like an old rag. Am I too exhausted to begin to love again? Maybe I dined on too many microwaved dishes while watching the news on TV. My mother used to sing Piaf, *Sans amour on n'est rien du tout*. Impossible to get that sentence out of my brain. *Without love we're nothing*. Yet God knows Tony's love made me unhappy and René's even more and even my minor loves let me down: Marcel and his poetry, Noël and his hash pipe. The only love that lasts, I told myself, is the love of my daughters and the friendship of Violette and Martine. How I wish I could duplicate with a man that unconditional love with no jealousy, no possessiveness, made up of hope and admiration! And I'm in the early stages of my already mad love for the baby who is splashing about in Sandra's womb, who will be born north of the North. How can I find with a man such fervour who won't let me down, who doesn't languish over time? What is it in love that kills us?

Time passed and the taxi was advancing in slow motion at the end of a line of headlights, unfurling as a long ribbon in the night that enclosed us like a cocoon. What time is your plane, Madame? I replied, it's probably landed already, I'm late, but it doesn't matter, we'll go there anyway. In the silent odour of the cigarette that the driver was smoking, I thought, I wanted to be a singer or an actress and I taught grade three. Tony and I thought we'd get rich and I don't have a cent. I'd have liked to travel and I stayed home. I have a plane ticket for Scotland in my purse, what's to stop me leaving for Aberdeen tonight? I would only have to say, Departures. I won't say it, I know that. How are people able to match their desires with reality? I can't do it. And now I'm hesitating to meet a man who's madly in love with me, *I'm crazy*, he wrote.

The stream of traffic was moving at a more normal rate and soon we'd arrived at the airport. All I wanted to do was go home and read my mother's letters. But when I saw the runway lit up for arrivals, all of a sudden I wanted to fly away, to purge myself of everything with no baggage, no house, no family.

It was nearly half past eight when the driver let me off in front of the big doors of the airport. I rushed to the arrivals gate, sure there would be no one in the waiting area near the baggage carousels. He'll have done what all the others on the Open Heart Line did, he'll have taken off when he saw that I wasn't there. I didn't mind being late. I wouldn't have to feel guilty, I could tell him about the surprise brunch, my daughters, the bad weather, the snow. If he ever calls me, I thought to myself.

There was no one in the arrivals area, except one tall man I saw from behind, gripping the telephone in a booth. He turned around when he heard my footsteps, he was the spitting image of François Rajotte from Winnipeg. My heart skipped three beats, I smiled at him. He said, Are you Katie? I answered, Maybe.

The sun rose a little earlier this morning. My mother used to say, More light every day after Epiphany. François is still asleep in my bedroom while I write in my journal, with Ravel's "Bolero" playing softly in the background. I'm on my third coffee. I've even written a little poem that I'll put on the table when I leave.

The typeface used in this book is Sabon, designed by Jan Tschichold and named after Jakob Sabon, who was a student of Claude Garamond.

Sabon was produced in 1964 by three foundries coming together to create a typeface that was consistent regardless of whether metal type composition, linecasting, or single-type machine composition was used.

Laced with a classical and elegant style, the readability of Sabon is a joy.